Bringing Ararat

Armand Inezian

A collection of short fiction

Last Light Studio
Boston, MA

2010

ISBN 10: 0982708408
ISBN 13: 9780982708408

Last
Light

a last light contemporary title.

Contents

The Lord Moves Us Forward, Forward

The Lord Moves Us Forward, Forward first appeared in The Western Humanities Review.

The organist, on the evening of our Grandmother Selma's death, was playing a 19th century Baptist tune, *The Lord Moves Us Forward, Forward*, on his aged pipe organ. This was an odd choice, it has been mentioned, for an Armenian Orthodox wedding, but a small amount of research shows that our parents' generation wasn't interested in maintaining a strong ethnic past. Mostly, they were interested in turning Watertown into a business district, setting up shop; and we, the grandchildren, were busy becoming fans of the Red Sox, Wonderbread, and Elvis. *The Lord Moves Us Forward, Forward* was considered to have mainstream appeal. It wasn't ethnic. Further, it was one of the best in the repertoire of Mr. Dzidzian "Sid" Cherkerzian, our organist. Sid was something of a minor celebrity in the Northeast, with his shiny hair and slick fingers, playing churches in the winter and Armenian vacation camps in the summer.

So play on Sid, please, because we need the organist for our story, much in the same way that an old western needs a piano player. Because when we get together, we compulsively, inevitably come back to the story of how Grandmother Selma died on the day of Aunty Anni's wedding, and your music helps ease our memories, as though the things we remember are not quite real.

"Medz Mama Selma. She was a character," we say thirty years later. We meet at Haig's house in Peabody. Haig, Jack's son, who forged himself a successful career in advertising sales, moved out to a fancy condo in Peabody, and who has come across as a bit of an ass ever since. After he forces us to watch the slideshow of his St. Lucia vacation, we sip our vodka or slivovitz and remember. "Selma! What a character." The subject is unavoidable; the story engrammed in our heads.

"I hated her," says Irena, Haykush's daughter. "I still have the scar on my ear."

Cara, Irena's sister who went to med school, says that she feels sorry for Selma. "She was crazy, but they didn't have a name for that kind of crazy back then."

Diggran's son, Antranig, just laughs and throws his hands up, "She was a Medz Mama! What do you expect?"

In Haig's living room, with its substantial wood detail and giant plasma screen, we reflect.

Sid and Aunty Anni and the priests- all of us- had come for a wedding and not to see a cross, old woman die. We don't say this out of resentment.

No, this is a lie. We do resent Selma. We can't help it. Selma was a gogortiloz, crocodile, of a woman. Mean, tough, and old-country as they came. She spent twenty-two years in America and never learned much more English than, "Yes, cigarette please," and "I need taxi now." In Armenian, however, she waxed monstrous, scaring us with her stories: The Mad Turk, The Dogs that Ate Children, The Sadana. She walked quickly, usually bent forward and accompanied by a hint of cigarettes and black pepper. She spanked the girls with her hand and whupped the boys with a wooden spoon. But these things were not unique; ask anyone over age fifty. What gives us special reason to resent her was the bitter fury she directed at Anni.

Selma had two daughters and two sons. In the traditional way, she favored the sons. The eldest, Diggran, is legendary for never having done a household chore in his life. Selma married Diggran off to Lena Hagopian, a subservient, fat woman, of the Battery Street Hagopians who owned the Yerevan Bakery. After the wedding, they both moved back into Grandmother Selma's home, switching from Diggran's bedroom to the in-law apartment. We remember Lena, Sundays after church, picking out Diggran's Monday clothes.

Jack, whose given name was Kersam, and Haykush were the middle children who, by virtue of their place in the birth line-up, efficiently Americanized and modernized.

And finally Anni, whom we remember as beautiful, with brown hair and a curvy figure. Tight dresses and black shoes. By current standards, Anni would be labeled too round to be beautiful. But we've found photographs of her, mostly shot between the early sixties and mid-seventies, and seeing her curvaceous ass in a tight spaghetti-strap dress still makes us blush. Photos of her in her wedding gown make us sigh. Anni was the youngest by far, and Selma had declared, based on custom, that Anni would stay home to cook and clean until Selma died.

Selma had begun to go crazy in her mid-40's, a few years after Anni was born. Not outright mad but more of a brooding kind of bitter. Our grandfather's death, about a decade later, brought her craziness out in relief. Prone to insomnia, she changed bedrooms often, shuffling her children around the house about twice a year, at one point lodging Jack in the stuffy, unfinished attic. She developed a habit of staring at babies, even in public, and in 1968, she was nearly arrested for grabbing an infant from the arms a passing woman on Commonwealth Ave. In 1969, she found Irena, age four, petting a stray cat and pulled her ears so hard that Irena's left earlobe ripped. Once Anni reached high school, Selma forbade her from leaving the house after six pm. Christmas of that year, she declared, at a large family gathering, that she would bury Anni alive if she lost her virginity. For us, the big-eyed grandchildren, there was no doubt as to who was Cinderella and who was the Wicked Grandmother.

Finally, there were stairs. In particular, the wooden, well-carpeted oak-board stairwell between the first and second floors of the old family home.

As kids, when we first heard the story of Selma hurling herself down the stairs, we laughed, but after we saw purple bruises on her old-lady face we felt as guilty and frightened as our parents.

Selma first threw herself down at age fifty-three. Of us, only Irena was there to witness the event. Irena will recount the story whenever we visit Uncle Diggran and Aunty Lena, who inherited the old home. Irena looks at the stairs "We were all going to the Cape for a weekend trip. Medz Mama Selma was already half crazy, so Uncle Diggran and Uncle Jack decided it would be better if she stayed home."

"Oh, don't blame me," Uncle Diggran protests, but he leans on his cane and looks as charmed as the rest of us, as though he somehow hadn't been there when that first tumble took place.

"Selma was standing on the second floor landing with a basket of laundry against her hip, and when they told her she couldn't go, she started throwing the laundry at us. To make her feel better, Uncle Jack tried to make up some big story about how the sun would irritate Selma's skin. Then she threw herself down the stairs. Thud! Thud! Just like that. She busted her lip and twisted an ankle. That blood

stain stayed on the carpet for years." Irena points to the spot.

Uncle Digrran does a tired old man laugh, shaking his head, and Antranig laughs along with his father.

"She wasn't always so strange, you know," Aunty Lena says, but we don't acknowledge this statement.

"None of us got to go to the Cape that year," Irena finishes. "We wound up taking Selma to the doctor and waiting around to make sure she was okay. By that time, no one felt like going anymore."

"Selma was nice, aghvor, a long time ago," Lena says again. "I remember when I was young, she used to bake bread for all the children on the street. She would serve it hot from the oven with raisins and butter. It was wonderful."

Cara, the doctor, nods, maybe in sympathy, but the rest of us hold our tongues.

Over the next few years, Selma became an expert at navigating those steps. When any of her children decided to move out, when Jack took a job at a firm that was too Jewish for her liking, or Haykush decided she'd had enough, Selma would throw herself down. She could read the warp and angle of the timber and find the carpeted spots with her eyes shut. Like a stuntwoman, she learned how to tuck her knees, elbows, shoulders and neck in so that she could roll at a good speed and still hit the sweet spots. She had the acumen of a pro wrestler. She could play those stairs the same way that Sid the Organist could tickle the ivories.

It was around the time of the stairs that Anni rebelled. She had cut her hair short and started wearing dark make-up. She met Garo Miradjanian, a vet with a minor disability, a metal plate in his leg. Garo had a motorcycle and smoked like mad. We were scared of him. We followed him everywhere. One night, some of us lay flat on a third floor balcony, hidden amongst chair legs and a few storages boxes, watching Garo kiss Anni, framed by amber streetlight and tobacco smoke, his fingers gently pressing at her cleavage.

Immediately, Selma understood the threat that Garo held. She said that they would never get married. She threatened suicide. She screamed and contorted. Once we saw her topless, her breasts not unlike punching bags, chasing Anni down the block with a clothing iron. After, we knew the wedding would be inevitable.

For a few months, Uncle Diggran tried to play peacemaker. He had started to make it big in the baked goods market and had the money to hire a full-time nurse and caretaker for Selma. The nurse's name was Mary Kaley. She had a stony face with red cheeks, and spoke with a high pitched girly-voice. Selma referred to Mary Kaley as the ter-chun aghcheeg, bird girl, because of Mary's high voice. Mary Kaley did an excellent job, the best she could considering the nature of her charge. She cleaned up after meals, drove Selma to the grocery store, watched her carefully on the stairwell, and put up with considerable verbal abuse, which thankfully she couldn't understand because it was all in Armenian, for four months before leaving for a hospital job downtown.

In the end, we suspect that it was Selma's unwillingness to address Mary Kaley directly that drove her to seek employment elsewhere. We remember Grandmother Selma drawing us aside and saying, in Armenian, "Tell the bird girl to hang up my coat."

After Mary Kaley left us, chore duties fell back on Aunt Anni, and it only took a few weeks before Anni, in her purple eye shadow, announced that she would marry dark and sexy Garo. We all were in the first floor dining room over plates of steaming dolmha, and after Anni made her announcement, Haykush and Jack ran like madmen to keep Selma from climbing the stairwell, but they weren't fast enough. Selma hurled herself down, wailing out loud.

As she tumbled, Haykush, who could swing a temper, kept calling Selma an old bitch. There was a rhythmic repetition that we remember:

Ka-chunk

Old Bitch

Ka-chunk

Old Bitch

When she finally hit the bottom, Grandmother Selma trembled as she stood, her hair a grey bird's nest. "You will not marry that man," she said. "Three thousand years and Moses, you will not marry that man!"

Sometimes, we secretly hope that Selma was just an evil witch who caught a fitting end, rather than a victim of biology and history because, as Haig the ad-man puts it, "Having to pity that woman, retroactively, would require a hell of a lot of leg work."

Cara the doctor, who has two children of her own, sometimes confesses to lying awake at night, hoping that whatever had gripped Grandmother Selma's head was not genetic.

We know that Cara might be right; that Selma would have had a better chance if she had been born fifty years later. Selma lived in Man's world. Maybe there was no healthy way to express her needs and feelings, whatever they might have been, in the Sixties. Maybe a high school diploma would have made some small difference. Maybe, born fifty years later, she would have had the chance to shave her head and dance to the Circle Jerks, or be diagnosed with bipolar disorder or chronic depression, or go sky diving, or gone on to love another man or whatever would have helped calm her madness. Then our thoughts travel to Aunty Anni who now lives quietly, divorced of course, in Michigan, and we worry about heredity.

The family quickly concluded that Anni's wedding would have to take place in a church with no stairs. When that proved impossible, they convinced the church office to keep all the doors to the stairwells locked for the duration of the ceremony.

Anni wore a simple, low-cut dress that left a lot of skin showing. It made her appear contradictorily innocent and sultry. Garo looked brilliant and brooding, like Rudolf Valentino, in his black tux. The two would ride off to the honeymoon on his motorcycle. To children who were starting to show some ambivalent interest in the other sex, it was enchanting.

"Seeing them together like that, wow! It was my first erection," Haig jokes when he's in that type of mood.

We don't like to think about events afterward, because it complicates things. Anni and Garo had a stormy relationship, which we didn't learn about until most of us had left for college. They fought hard and bitter. They moved to Michigan where Garo could work for a motorcycle concern, and lost contact with the family. A few years after that, Garo left her for another woman. Anni was diagnosed with depression and began therapy.

Anni stayed in Michigan. She doesn't come back to Watertown and only returns calls in a sort of noncommittal way on major holidays. We hope she is as beautiful as ever, but we hear her smoker's cough and imagine her eyes are big and hollow and tired. Maybe we don't want to see her anyway. Is she still in heavy eyeliner? She never went to college. Michigan winters make people fat. Maybe she'll remind us too much of Medz Mama Selma.

We would rather hold on to the magic that the wedding seemed to promise. A bit of a happy ending. We'll go back there- to the ceremony.

Sid played for us. Still does, in our minds. We remember him. His pomaded hair and winning smile. His slender fingers. He was known for *The Lord Moves us Forward, Forward* which he played with love, depth, and a quickness at Aunt Anni's wedding. We knew the words. We still do; it's a popular tune. Some of us sang along.

The Lord moves us forward,

Forward

Into the valley of joy

And joyfully we go onward

Forward

Singing Praise on him we go.

Thankfully, Selma seemed a bit tired and withdrawn. She was low-key during the ceremony, but we kept an eye on her.

The Armenian Orthodox priest, with his long beard and velvet robes, chanted in old Armenian, which we could scarcely follow save for the triple recitation of Der Voghormia, Der Voghormia, Der Voghormia which we understood as the Armenian way of saying Hallelujah. We tilted our heads back to catch glimpses of the cathedral ceiling, painted sky blue with murals depicting half-naked men and women going about the mighty business of religion: crucifixion, temptation, baptism.

The girls watched the audience, carefully noting each family member's reaction to the ceremony. The boys watched Anni's bosom- you could just see it through her veil- which rose eagerly with each breath. Our parents, uncles, and aunts were now focused entirely on the ceremony. That's when Selma must have walked out.

Unbeknownst to any of us, except for God maybe, if He was in the house- Selma had left her seat and found a service stairwell to the basement. In order to do this, she had to leave the actual congregation and walk out a side exit. The stairs were waiting for her, long, lean and made of unforgiving stone. It was a steep drop-off, vanishing into darkness.

We think life is unfair, and we think it holds marvels. Among us, we have a feminist, a Marxist, a historical reconstructionist, and a postmodern deconstructionist. And a few of us simply fall into the camp known as, "Medz Mama was fucking crazy." But these perspectives hardly matter. Or they only matter to a certain point. We all have the same picture in our heads- like the waking end of a dream, the image of a chubby, stuffy woman in an ill-fitting formal gown tumbling, like a porcelain doll, rolling into the darkness until we can no longer see the steps, and it appears as though she is floating or flying away.

We remember. Dzidzian "Sid" Cherkerzian stared at the keys of his organ, not playing, and flicked a stray bang from his forehead. The priest paused for just a second. Aunt Anni took a shimmering breath; her future, for the moment, was bright. We wondered when our turns would come. We, the grandchildren, looked at each other. We noticed that Selma was gone. We figured there was plenty of time to dwell on her disappearance. We held our tongues.

See Me

See Me first appeared in Glimmer Train

The night had been slow, and that worried him, because he didn't like to be left alone with thoughts and memories. If there had been a better place to go, he would have closed down the shop and left, but there wasn't. He had to wait for the boy anyway. So Calust was relieved when Dr. Higgenbotham, a tanned, older practitioner who kept late hours, came in for a trim, which kept him busy until his nephew rolled his bike into the shop. The boy, as usual, had an entire video game system tucked into his backpack. He wore a shirt that said *Douchebag For Hire*.

"*Douchebag inche?*" Calust asked him in Armenian.

The boy shook his head. "English, Uncle Cal. English." He methodically unpacked the game. "It's the language of the future."

"What means this Douchebag For Hire?"

The boy pulled at the lower corners of his shirt. "You don't know what this is? Then you don't need to know. It's on a need-to-know basis." As always, the boy was full of himself, but Calust noticed a thin hint of blush on Hal's face.

His nephew's given name wasn't Hal, it was Hovig, but he hadn't let anyone call him that since he was eight years old, and that pretty much spelled things out for Calust. Hal was an only child, a late-in-life child, spoiled by Arpi and Ken when they were together and made further rotten by their ongoing divorce, or maybe it was the boy's age - Calust and Taline had been unable to have children, so they remained something a of a mystery to him - Hal was fourteen. Americanized as could be, he hadn't discovered girls but had discovered anarchy symbols, the underground, irony, bathroom humor. His big, brown eyes reminded Calust of his own father, and Hal used those eyes to throw pained glances. He was big-footed, tall and thin with a taste for baggy clothes which made him look even more gawky and had recently taken to wearing disturbing t-shirts- one of Calust's least favorites had a photograph of a male chimpanzee with its genitals splayed, front and center- didn't want to learn a lick of Armenian, and now he'd become Calust's part-time problem.

"Can I play my game?" Hal asked flatly.

"Yes, but you should keep the noise-volume low."

"You don't have to say noise-volume, Uncle Cal. You can just say volume, it means the same thing."

"And there is sesame candy under the counter if you like."

"Do you have any chocolate?" Hal coiled loops of cable around the back of the TV.

"Is that your boy?" Higgenbotham finally asked.

"No sir. He is my sister's."

"I would never let any son of mine wear that shirt. Not

while he was under my roof."

Calust stared at his nephew who seemed lost in his game. "His family is having troubles. He is a smart boy but with little to do." He sprinkled talc onto a towel and ran it over Higgenbotham's balding head.

"Still," Higgenbotham insisted.

"Yes. I know it is only a matter of time before he gets the nostril ring."

"The nostril ring!" Hal cackled.

"Yerp hyren lav kitnaas, ayn adeneh ghu ghoseenk."

"What? Why don't you learn English? You've been here for –like- fifty years. That's almost four times as long as I've been alive," and before Calust could think of a clever reply in Armenian, or less clever in English, the boy was reabsorbed into his game.

Higgenbotham leaned forward in the chair so Calust could wipe the back of his neck. "Take care of that boy well," he said. "You never know what sort of trouble obnoxious boys might get into. Especially as they grow up."

"Yes. Thank you, Doctor." He finished with Higgenbotham, made a count of the cash drawer and then stared at Hal who sat, Indian style, on the reception bench, furiously mashing his fingers against the game controller. "Hal, when is your mother coming?"

"Oh, now you speak English?"

"Did your mother say she was coming at eight?"

"Eight-thirty."

Calust climbed into one of his vinyl-backed customer chairs and closed his eyes. There was nothing to do but wait, he knew. These days, waiting was something he disliked because it made him realize how much time he had on his hands, and how time was being filled with old memories, sunken ships that unearthed themselves from the ocean floor, floated back up and resurfaced in unnervingly vivid swells of light, sound and color. These old memories- the tastes of candies of his youth, pictures of rooms on other continents, the smell of long-defunct brands of hair tonic, conversations with relatives who'd died decades ago- who needed them? Only a few nights before, he'd woken with a gasp as he heard the distinct mouse-like squeak of the old mattress that he had slept on in Bucharest fifty years before. *Don't think too hard- shad parageh mi medadzer-* he reminded himself. It was something that his father used to say.

Uncle Krikor. It had been pitch black until he had lit a candle on the table between them. Krikor, already a good-looking man with curly black hair and bee-stung lips, had looked like a movie star in the golden light. "Quiet," he had whispered, "and you will come to know the ancient secrets of our family."

Despite understanding that his uncle was a showman, a penny-ante magician, Calust got the chills that any ten year old might under the circumstances. Krikor offered shadows and drama.

"Are you ready, Calust?"

He nodded.

"Taqorian is your last name. Do you knows what that means?"

"Taqorian," Calust repeated, lost as to what his role in all this was.

"Think about it. What is taqavor?"

"King!"

His uncle flashed one of many trademark smiles.

"But, if we are the sons of kings, then why don't we have money? Why do you and Papa cut hair?"

"Our family's fortune was lost in old wars, so we learned the trade of cutting hair. Not that there is any shame in learning a trade. Because when you cut a man's hair, you are giving him a crown to wear, making him king for a day.

"Let me tell you a story of our ancestors, emperors from long ago. They amassed great wealth, which they kept in a fort on Mount Ararat. The treasure was guarded by scarred men with iron spears. Not just men, but trained lions and eagles as well."

"Liar!"

Krikor laughed, but then he shushed Calust. "Will you offend the spirits of our dead ancestors? Do you know that their ghosts watch you every second of your life?"

"Not true."

"Do not offend them or they will become corporeal and snatch your heart and breath. The dead are jealous of the living, and if you give them good reason, they will pull you down. Do you know what it is like down there? It's made of hot, acid fog. There are no landmarks, nothing to guide yourself by. You will simply wander, forever, among grey ghosts, and the fog will burn and sting. Over time, it will melt your eyes and your skin. You won't have any food, so you will grow skinny until your ribs stick out from beneath your rotten flesh."

Calust went silent, aware of the dark all around.

"I know they are real because I see them in dreams. I see them, and it's as though someone has turned my eyes inside out." Krikor seemed to be speaking more to himself than to Calust. Krikor's eyes closed as though he might fall asleep at that moment and have those very dreams, and behind him the door burst open, flooding the room with light. The silhouette of a man confronted them, and it took Calust a breathless moment to realize it was his own father.

His father half-stumbled past a box looking for the light switch. "What are you doing in the dark? Calust? Krikor- we have five customers waiting."

"I was just entertaining your son, Ardash." Krikor gave a cross-eyed grin that always made him look drunk. He gently punched Calust on the shoulder as he ambled back out onto the shop floor.

Calust studied his father, who was quite a bit older than Krikor, and the thinning hair, bristly mustache and constant look of tired reserve made Calust wonder how these two men could have come from the same mother. He hoped, as he aged, he would look less like his father and more like his uncle.

"And if you are done with your studies, then I need you to sweep the floor."

"I'm not done with my studies," Calust mumbled.

"You will sit down in that chair and finish then," his father said in his low voice to indicate he was serious.

"Yes, Papa." Calust reopened his math book and sharpened his pencil. He felt his father's stare against his back.

"What did he tell you?" Ardash asked.

"Nothing."

"Nothing?"

"About ghosts. He was telling scary stories."

Ardash stood at the threshold for one more second and then went back into the shop. Through the half-open door, Calust could see his father speaking to Krikor in a low voice so that customers couldn't hear. They were arguing, Calust guessed, something they often did. Despite recurring tensions, however, the two brothers complimented each other in business. Ardash was the responsible one. He kept the books, worked with grim-faced determination, and constantly cleaned. And Krikor was the salesman. He joked with the customers and flirted with any ladies who came by. And if Krikor had bad traits, like his habit of disappearing when there was work to be done, Ardash had flaws as well: his stubborn unwillingness to chat with customers, his knee-jerk prejudice against Russians and Jews, the grunting noise he sometimes made instead of saying *hello*.

Calust had watched them a moment more. Then he had cheated his chair over to get under the light and gone back to basic algebra. "Six times X is twenty four," he had whispered all those decades ago. "Such that X is four. Such that X marks the spot of the land of the dead."

Arpi was low on cash because of the divorce, so she drove herself hard on nights and weekends. Having come directly from a showing, she was still in a navy pant-suit, her hair with blond highlights, a fresh coat of lipstick and a bite-the-bullet smile. She often carried that smile, and it made Calust unsure of whether the divorce was a relief or if she was hiding her true feelings. Either way, it made him nervous. "Thank you for watching him, Cal," she said in Armenian.

He kissed his sister formally on the cheek. He wanted to inquire about the state of the divorce, but was unsure of how to ask. "So, you must have sold the house," he said instead.

"Oh, it's not that simple. You can't sell a house in one night. Has he been good?"

"He hasn't moved except to use the toilet and go around the corner for soda."

"Hi Mom," Hal glanced at her. "I'm almost going to kill the leader of the aliens." The TV screen swirled in a mix of cartoon gunfire, body parts and alien monsters.

"Can you take him on Sunday?" Arpi asked. "I have a three open houses I can't miss, and Ken is still at his parents'."

Calust didn't know what to make of the fact that she still kept track of her soon-to-be ex-husband's movements. "I don't know," he said.

"Take him to a movie. He loves movies. It will be a nice time for the both of you."

He tried to think of some way to refuse Arpi's request, some excuse he might give, but he had no plans and Arpi knew it, so he was honest. "There's nothing for us to talk about. I don't think he cares to spend time with me."

"Calust," she said with mild exasperation, "you'll be watching the show, so you don't even have to talk."

"But people like to talk about the movie afterwards. No?" It had been years since he'd been to a film but he remembered that, when they had been younger, Taline and he would follow movies with Turkish coffee and spend the evening discussing the things they'd liked, and what they hadn't, and whether they wanted to see it again.

"That's not how it is with children these days. They don't want to talk to adults. They only want to talk to other kids. Will you do this for me, Cal?"

Calust owed his sister. After Taline had succumbed to cancer, he'd had a breakdown. A quiet one, but a breakdown nevertheless. He'd been overcome with headaches and frequent insomnia. Far worse was the feeling that he'd suddenly lost perspective on people, places and events, so that he had trouble remembering the faces of customers who'd regularly come to his Manhattan shop, so that he had trouble recalling conversations he'd had with Taline. Time became a sloppy element. He couldn't sleep at night. Sometimes the days seemed endless.

"Come to Simi," Arpi had urged him over the phone almost three years before.

"Come to see you?"

"Not *see me*- Simi! Simi Valley."

"What is Simi Valley?"

"It's where we live. We moved last year, remember? You'll like it. It's near the desert and warm. Near LA, but not so congested."

"See me," Calust had said under his breath.

He'd felt anchorless and had let Arpi talk him into relocating. She and Ken had housed, fed, and kept him in clean clothes for almost a year. She'd helped him find the Singers' house and a shop to lease. And Hal had been there too, but the boy was smaller and quieter back then and the truth was that Calust had been far too remote to really engage the boy. In a moment of sympathy, Calust realized that he must have seemed like a strange, foreign lodger to Hal back then.

Of course, the move had brought about an unforeseen batch of issues. Calust found himself uprooted from his few remaining friends and acquaintances and in a home he never quite felt comfortable in. He'd given up the lease on a much more profitable shop, their father's, in Manhattan. And, as time went by, he realized that Simi Valley wasn't a California paradise like in the movies, but smoggy, hot and overpaved on the outside and vacuum-sealed from within.

Simi lacked things he'd taken for granted: big buildings, watercourses, taxi cabs, hole-in-the-wall cafes, people talking on corners, and policemen on horses. He felt as though this was the place to be if you wanted to slowly fade away and not inconvenience anyone as you did so.

Nevertheless, he clearly owed Arpi. "I'll take him to a movie then, but I will not see some ridiculous Hollywood film ," he jabbed a finger at her for emphasis. "I want to see a film with good acting and a nice story."

"You would be better off letting the boy see what he wants. He'll be less of a headache," she suggested.

"And I don't want him wearing any of those embarrassing shirts."

Arpi switched to English which, unlike Calust's, had only a trace of an accent. "Hal, Uncle Cal is going to watch you on Sunday. He's going to take you to the movies."

"Okay," Hal said, "but no boring foreign films, okay?"

He fished mail from the Singers' vinyl mailbox. Legally, of course, the house belonged to Calust, but in many ways it was still the Singers'. Arpi had convinced him to buy the place furnished - it would save him time and energy, she said - but the unintended consequence was that Calust always felt like a guest. The couch, the pavers along the driveway, the color schemes, the rugs, even the toaster were the Singers', and now that their forwarding period had ended, the junk mail came in their name too. He threw most of it out, keeping only a bill from the Department of Water and

Power. "Water is power," he said to himself, an expression he'd picked up from one of his customers.

He'd spent the drive home trying to figure from where the sudden memory of Uncle Krikor had come. Why had it come on so strong? At first he had guessed that it had to do with the presence of his own nephew, Hal. But the truth was that Hal was often at the shop, which had become his surrogate after-school care center. Then he had realized it was the old scissors that he'd used on Higgenbotham. A simple pair made of forged iron with a loop for the thumb, they looked very much like the pair that Krikor had used. In fact, he recalled how Krikor had showed him a magic trick that involved using wax and fishing line to make it appear as though the scissors – he would spin them quickly in low light - were levitating of their own accord. Calust had tried to teach himself the trick as a young man, but he'd never quite been able to master it. And with Krikor gone, there had been no one to ask.

He threw the water bill on the coffee table as he walked in. The living room smelled faintly of overhot upholstery. "The magic scissors," he mumbled to himself. He turned on the central air and watched some talk show people on the Singers' TV. Putting his feet up on the couch, he decided he would probably sleep there rather than going to bed. He took off his shoes and socks and stared at old-man feet; the skin stretched tight, age spots. One of his smaller toes, broken many years before while scrambling down a stairwell to dodge a mugger, sat at a strange angle. He lay his head back, the TV show now mostly blurry wallpaper, and he was well aware that some small part of his mind continued to spin, fighting sleep. He thought of Uncle Krikor's scissors, spinning, dancing, the cold metal reflecting light. He'd never been able to replicate it. *Don't think so hard,* he reminded himself. It was something his father would say when they used to argue. But memory came.

They had come for Uncle Krikor. Just after dark, plainclothes policemen had come to their home in the Armenian ghetto of Bucharest. Calust had been in his room; he'd spent the evening sketching magicians. "Calust!" His father called from down the hall. "Come out." Two men dressed in grey suits with black overcoats. One was fat and doughy. His forehead was peppered with odd birthmarks. The other man was younger with blond hair and a mustache. Calust stared at them in the naked way that children can. He saw bulges in their coats. "They have guns," he whispered.

The fat one smiled at him in a not-unkind way, then said to Calust's father in Romanian, "This is your entire family? Everyone?"

"My wife. My children. My mother-in-law."

The fat man pulled a slip of paper from his coat pocket. "And your brother is Krikor Taqorian?"

Ardash nodded.

"He lives here."

"No," Ardash lied. "He recently moved in with my cousin. They are in Constanta."

"This is his registered address." The fat man checked his slip of paper again. "Right here."

Never much for talk, Ardash said nothing. He sat down in his overstuffed chair and stared at the floor.

"He does live here, I believe. And I believe that we will wait here until he comes."

Ardash shook his head.

It wasn't unusual for Krikor, who was out on a date, to stay out late, so they waited hours. The two policemen kept vigil near the door. Ardash hardly moved. Calust's mother made tea but didn't offer any to the policemen. And his grandmother held baby Arpi. Calust chewed on his lip and stared, first at the policemen and then at then at his parents. Nothing happened, and his initial confusion faded to antsy frustration. He drank three cups of hot tea and then announced, "I have to pee!" The bathroom was outside, down the hall.

"I will take him," his mother said.

"No," the blond policeman said. "You stay. I'll do it."

They walked down the long, beige hall. Some families made a practice of keeping their doors open, and they stared openly at the blond man escorting the small, curly-headed boy. Lala Jafarian, who was a crazy old woman and could get away with such things, came out of her apartment and made the sign of the cross in the blond man's face. It was at that moment, watching Lala's skinny, ivory fingers, that Calust understood the weight of the situation. He suddenly felt as though someone had filled his stomach with hot air. He felt fear, hate, fantasies of escape. He kept his eyes on the floor.

"Well, pee now," the policeman said when they arrived at the toilet.

He couldn't. He looked up at the blond man, memorizing his face. He was a handsome man. His mustache nicely groomed and- Calust noticed this because of his own father's bristly mustache- just a little waxed. The man's eyes were brown and evenly spaced. His teeth seemed to fit tightly in his mouth. The butt of his gun was just visible under his coat. "If you're not going to pee, then we're going back."

"Wait!" Then Calust spit out that one curse word he knew in Romanian and immediately froze as he realized what he'd said.

The policeman looked at him, thinned his lips. "I could kill you," he said, flashing his revolver, but he let Calust stand over the toilet, and they remained for almost two full minutes before Calust finally released.

"It's about time."

"You know, my uncle is a magician. You can never arrest him."

"I thought you were Armenians," the blond man said, "not Gypsies. Let's take you back."

And when Krikor had finally came home in his black tuxedo with a lipstick smear on the collar, he had looked like some kind of magician. He saw the police officers and smiled in a crazy way, as though he'd stumbled into a surprise party. "Hello!" he said. He made a small gesture toward the ceiling and then hung his jacket over the crook of his arm.

"Krikor Taqorian," said the fat one.

"No." Krikor said.

Simultaneously, the two men rushed him, and Krikor resisted for a few seconds, he spun and tried to make his way back to the door, but they cuffed his wrists. Calust's mother yelled at the policemen, and his grandmother, who'd remained quiet throughout the night, began to pray out loud. Ardash stood up in front of the cops. "Krikor," he said.

"That's not my name," Krikor grinned in a pained way.

"I'm coming with you," Ardash said. He rushed to grab his coat.

"Suit yourself," said the fat one.

"We'll sort this out," Krikor said, generally to everyone, which was the last thing Calust ever heard him say.

They spent most of the night waiting for his father to return, and when he did, Ardash's face was dark with shadows under his eyes and stubble. Calust was told to watch Arpi as the adults cloistered themselves, whispering, in the kitchen.

"What did they want?" Calust asked when they finally came out.

"Not now," Ardash said.

"What happened to Uncle Krikor? Is he in prison?" He sat up, went to his father.

"We've had too many troubles tonight. I'll tell you, but not now," But that was a lie. His father would never explain what had happened. Ardash put his hand on his son's shoulder, offering reassurance but also keeping Calust from getting any closer. Ardash was quiet for some time, and then he said, "Everyone is leaving this place. We need to leave this place too."

When he came to pick up Hal, Calust found the boy wearing the infamous naked chimpanzee shirt, and demanded to speak to Arpi or even Ken. Hal reminded him that neither parent was there, which was why Calust had been asked to baby-sit in the first place. "You are hardly a baby. Now change your shirt, please," said Calust. Which, as it turned out, was a problem since every one of Hal's shirts sported a disturbing image: elephants mating, the album cover for a death-metal band, a fat man baring his ass. He couldn't believe that Arpi tolerated this and chalked it up to some permutation of divorce. Finally, from the bottom of his pajama drawer, Hal produced a plain blue t-shirt. "Is this okay?" He rolled his big eyes.

"There. That is nice. You look like a handsome boy now."

"I look like a boring boy."

As a way of rewarding Hal for changing shirts, Calust agreed to buy tickets to a gangster film that Hal wanted to see. He remembered seeing *The Godfather* with Taline when it was first released, and they both had been taken with the storyline and acting. This movie, however, was nothing like *The Godfather*. This movie involved shirtless, tattooed Asian and Black men fighting against some sort of drug cartel controlled by an evil general. Much of it was taken up with expensive automobiles, drug use, men being smashed in the face and young women's breasts, most of which, Calust was quite sure, were not meant to be seen by Hal.

"I liked it when that guy snapped the cybernetic guy's neck and his eyeballs popped out," Hal said as they walked back to the car. "I liked it when that girl, the blond one, showed her boobs with all those tattoos on them."

Even with his rough English and poor social skills, Calust could tell that the boy was trying to get a rise out of him, test his authority, so he continued toward the car without responding.

"You don't want to talk about it, Uncle Cal?"

"You are going home. I am driving you home." He started the car.

"My mom won't be home 'til five."

"We will go to the shop, then. You may play your games there."

"Why don't we just go to your house?"

"There is nothing to do there." Calust couldn't imagine having a guest in the house he barely felt comfortable in. They rode in silence for a while, passing knots of traffic, endless retail parking and pink-stucco subdivisions. The desert sun glared.

"You don't want to talk about the naked girl? Because they say that adults should talk about sex and violence with kids after they see those types of movies. You know, to help develop values. Right?" Hal spoke in a tone that suggested that he was simultaneously concerned with and mocking all things adult.

"You may wish to speak about such things with your mother."

And then Hal turned on the radio. He reached right over and turned it on full blast, switching stations until he found one that filled Calust's car with angry rock music.

Calust slapped Hal's hand aside and turned it off. "You are a rude child," he said. Part of him flinched as he realized that Hal had succeeded in getting that rise out of him, but the embarrassment quickly solidified to anger.

Hal threw his hands up, "What? You don't like my music? Everybody judges me!"

Calust spun the wheel and came to a grinding stop at the curb. "Everybody judges you? Who are you? Tell me, have you ever seen the lady's breasts?"

"*The* lady's breasts?" Hal laughed.

"Have you ever seen the breasts of a woman? Not in the magazine. Not in the video, but in life?"

Hal looked at him.

"Answer me," Calust let acid come up in his voice, something that he hadn't done since he, himself, had been a teenager fighting with his father. "The car stays here until you answer."

Hal crossed his arms. The air conditioning hummed softly.

"You are a child, Hovig. Because you have played video games and seen movies, you think you know about the world, but you don't know. I lived in Manhattan. I have been mugged more than once and my shop broken into many times. I have made love to my wife more times than you can think. Before that, I lived in Bucharest. I am a man of the world. And even my story is not as strange as my father's and my uncle's. And what do you know, Hovig? You know how to watch the TV."

Neither spoke as they drove back to the shop. Calust kept the *Closed* sign up and used the time to inventory wares. Hal sat down on the bench in the reception area, stared down at his oversize feet and moved his lips occasionally, possibly making some mute argument or cursing under his breath.

After nearly half an hour, the boy said, "Can I tell you about one part of the movie that I liked? I liked it when that Chinese guy went to Himalayas to learn the secret kung fu style, and they were all on top of that mountain with all the ancient temples and clouds and waterfalls."

Calust, who was in the middle of oiling clippers, said, "Yes. That was nice because it is nice to believe that there are such places that you may go and find isolation and peace. Places where you don't have to deal with others."

"And you don't have to deal with all the chaos," Hal said. "I'd like to go to a mountain like that."

"That would be nice. Maybe I would go with you."

"Maybe."

"I am sorry I yelled at you, Hovig."

"Hal."

"I am sorry, Hal."

"It's okay. I'm over it," Hal mumbled. "I'm over."

Saturday pre-dawn, he woke in a sweat. His body felt hot and his muscles, limp. Within a moment, he was no longer afraid. In his dream, he'd been eight again. He had been talking with Uncle Krikor, who was speaking although his lips never moved. Something was closing in. An apparition. A fog. They were smothered in grey light.

He drank some juice from the Singers' fridge and took a cool shower. Then he carried a blanket to the sofa and turned on the late news and waited for the sun.

He went in early to the shop, which was quickly filled with young men from a construction crew. Some of them wanted buzz cuts and the rest- they'd apparently all come from coffee together- were hanging around before their day started. One of them standing near the front door kept repeating the f-word, and Calust was trying to find a polite way to ask him to stop when the phone rang. "He ran away," Arpi said, her voice pressed between urgency and irritation. "He didn't come home last night,"

"Hovig?"

"Hal, yes. He took his bicycle and didn't come back. I spent half the night driving around, looking. Is he with you?"

"No. Did you call Ken?"

"He didn't go to Ken. Ken was out looking too. When I find that boy, he'll be in big trouble."

Calust tried to imagine where a young man might go: video game parlors, sporting events or movies, maybe. He realized that, with the exception of the cinema he'd taken Hal to, he had no idea where any of those places might be. Suddenly he said, "I had a dream about people disappearing."

"What?"

"Uncle Kirkor. Do you remember him? You were very little."

"Was he the one who died in the war?"

"No, Krikor lived with us in Bucharest. He was taken by the police. Do you know the story?"

"Cal, why are you telling me this now? Are you trying to tell me that I'll never see Hal again?"

"No. No." But he realized, in a shameful way, that that was exactly why he'd thought to mention the dream. "I'm sorry, Arpi. I did not mean to suggest such a thing. Give me about half an hour," he said, "and I will help you look. Did you call the police?"

"The police," she said, her voice losing the edge it had carried a few moments before.

Moving fast, he finished off the buzz cuts and closed down the shop. He spent the day driving across Simi with the yellow pages and a map book in his car. He went from one shopping center to another, feeling lost. For the life of him, he could not recall the color of Hal's bike, and he'd never owned a mobile phone, so he had no way of checking in with Arpi. At each destination, he cruised the parking lot once and then went inside. He walked slowly through arcades, hobby shops and theater lobbies, weaving as best he could to get a better view of people as they passed. These places were dimly lit and noisy. Calust had no idea that so many children would be out without supervision.

It was only after he visited the cinema where they had seen the gangster movie that he remembered how Hal had talked about escaping to mountains. He knew there were hills and hiking trails to the north, and he decided to follow his instincts and drive out that way.

It was the early afternoon by the time he reached them, and the worst of the heat was sloughing off the land. He cracked open a window and drove up an old, winding road. Most of the landscape was chaparral with the occasional stray pine, eucalyptus or fig tree fortunate enough to have grown in a shady nook. He drove slowly, glancing out of both side windows. He caught occasional flashes of color: a lizard darting across the road, a yellow songbird, a sweaty power-jogger in an orange safety vest.

It went on for miles. At a higher elevation, the landscape became stony, the road reduced to a dirt path, and then it ended entirely. He finally stopped the car at a place that had evidence- cracked mud banks, patches of wild flowers- of being a dried-up pond. *Water is power*, he thought. Could Hal have come up here? He got out of the car. The sun was still high, but the air was cooler than in the valley. His shoes filling with sand and gravel, he crossed the dried pond to a hiking path. Far above, he could see a buzzard circling.

After about twenty minutes of walking, not sure of what to look for, he decided to scramble up to a nearby precipice that afforded him a panoramic view of the back side of the hills. The landscape there was brown and the sky a pale, blue lid that pushed down hard. Space felt compressed. Looking down into the next valley, he was surprised to see tall barrel-shaped cacti of the type he'd only seen in cowboy movies. Not only cacti, but- as he tracked a flicker of motion- a coyote as well. It was a scraggly, whip-like creature that darted across the landscape with its head bowed. Calust watched until it jogged over a small rise and was gone.

Having spent forty years in Manhattan, with its massive range of highrises and throngs of people, he always imagined that he understood the workings of space and how people spread through it, but here he found severe contrast. A huge landscape, simultaneously folded and flat. How easy it would be to get lost. Was the boy gone? It occurred to him that if Hal really wanted to vanish, if he was determined, he might disappear for good. He might. Sometimes, people went.

On his way back to the car, he spotted something on the ground. It looked like a dead animal until he got closer and saw that it was a backpack. He lifted it by a strap and held it up. Coated with fine dust, it might have been there a day or two. He brushed the bag off and saw that it was grey, and at that moment he realized, despite having seen it dozens of times, he couldn't recall the color of Hal's backpack. *Blue*, he thought. *It was blue.* But maybe it was black, or grey. How many other things about Hal did he not know and, vice-versa, how little did Hal know about him? Did people learn and remember only enough to get by? The idea bothered him.

He went through the pockets of the backpack searching for clues: a plastic zip-bag with the remnants of a sandwich, a pair of white athletic socks, a beat up CD player. It was unlikely that this was Hal's bag, Calust guessed, because the boy wouldn't just toss it aside. Not unless there had been extreme circumstances. He circled the ground looking for tracks or footprints but only found his own. There was nothing more to be done.

The revelation had come without warning, without fanfare or omens which, in light of his penchant for dramatic flare, would probably have been unsatisfactory for Uncle Krikor. Calust hadn't broached the topic in decades, not since he'd been a hot-headed teenager rebelling against his father, and so he was surprised that it somehow came back to the surface, this long-sunken ship, on a warm Sunday at a nursing home in Queens. On Taline's recommendation, he brought flowers, bright yellow daffodils.

"Oh, they are pretty," his mother said in Armenian.

He put the flowers on her bedside table and kissed her cheeks. "And how are you, Mama?"

"My back still hurts and my legs feel weak."

"I'll call the nurse."

"No, Calust, there's no need. My back always hurts, and my legs always feel weak."

He regarded her unhappily, and she must have sensed

this because she changed topics. "How are things at the hair parlor? Is it busy?"

"It's a little slower. Some of the regular customers moved to Florida. I need to advertise more. I had a few men come in this morning, and then I had lunch. After that, no one came, so you know what I did? I spent half an hour trying to make my scissors dance in the air."

"Why would you do that?"

He sat in the guest chair. "You remember how Uncle Krikor used to do that? Like a magic trick?"

She crumpled her face in concentration and then laughed. She seemed suddenly full of joy. "Krikor. What a wonderful boy."

"Then why didn't you do anything?" The question; it wasn't so much a question as a deep yearning. Where had it come from? It had come from out of nowhere with massive force, a rip tide.

"Calust, What are you talking about?"

"Krikor! He was arrested."

"You're angry."

"Do you remember what happened to him? He was arrested."

"I know he was arrested. I remember. You don't have to yell at your sick mother."

Her roommate, another elderly woman, stared at them, but he knew that it was unlikely that she understood any Armenian. "He was taken by the secret police, and you and

Papa, you both pretended that it never happened. As though he never existed."

She regarded him for a moment. "Get me a glass of water," she said.

He was as surprised as her by his outburst. As he filled her glass, he watched his mother closely. Her face had grown pale and long over time. Her eyes were, as always, the same merciful shade of hazel. He felt simultaneously righteous and sheepish. He thought it best to remain quiet.

After she took a sip of water, she said, "Your uncle was selling morphine on the black market. Not only that, but he had started taking the morphine himself. That's why the police came."

And there it was. A revelation that had come from nowhere, and yet he had to acknowledge that it had been out there, somewhere, building up for decades. How many times had he, as a red-faced boy, confronted his father about this? How many times had he pushed, pried and bothered? *Shad parageh mi medadzer.* And now, hearing his mother say this, decades after he'd given up, was like the first time, age twenty four, that he'd seen Taline naked. He felt as though his insides were made of delicate crystal, like he shouldn't move or breath too hard.

"He knew a soldier in the army," she said. "That soldier stole medical morphine. Krikor bought it from him and sold it around Bucharest, mostly to veterans who were addicted from the time of the War. It was a burden on your father. Twice a burden because we all loved Krikor. And because he lived with us, he put us all in jeopardy. Can you guess why your father would never tell you about this? It was obvious that you were devoted to your uncle. So don't just sit with that cold look on your face, Calust. You must have suspected something."

Calust shook his head. "He wouldn't tell me, not even years later."

"You know that Ardash was a stubborn man. He kept his feelings locked away. You know that, Calust."

"Nobody keeps their feelings locked in like that. Not unless they had something to hide"

"It's true. Your father blamed himself for losing his own brother. He warned him, but Krikor always acted like it was a joke, as though nothing bad could ever happen. He was too smart for his own good." Staring at her hands, she seemed to lose herself. Finally, she said, "He began to take the morphine. He acted strangely. He talked about doing violent things and started hiding drugs in the hair parlor. He said he was having visions. Sometimes, he would stand out on the street and talk to himself. We suspect it was this behavior that made it necessary for someone to call the police."

"Morphine," Calust said, letting the word set on his tongue.

"We never found out what happened to him. Ardash thought he might have been executed. He wasn't a common criminal. He was turned over to the military because the morphine had been stolen from the army. Your father tried to find information, but you know back then, with Ceausescu in office, they were hard on people who asked too many questions. In the end, we had to let go."

Calust waited, unsure if there was anything that he might say.

"People let go, Calust," she finally said.

"We did not let go, Mama. Krikor was taken."

"Sometimes," she said emphatically, "people let go. Calust, when you were young you used to complain that your father was mean and bitter, but now you look just like him except without the mustache. I see angry creases around your face. I can only hope you are nice to Taline."

"Of course I am."

"You are my son."

"Well, I know that."

"Good. Then you know something," she said. "And I hope you will stop worrying over your dead father and uncle."

He stood up. He felt scared, so he did not ask who'd actually called the police. It was Romania, a communist regime run by a madman. The secret police had worked hard to make sure that family informed on family. Sometimes it was the only way to survive. He straightened the creases in his pants. It might not have been his parents who'd told. It could easily have been neighbors, or even a stranger on the street. He kissed his mother goodbye. He did not ask.

He had walked out of the nursing home and into Spring air. There were traffic noises, people coming and going. Birds zipped over the avenue; above them, the tops of tall buildings, and above them, airplanes buzzing. Life went on. A well-dressed panhandler in a clean white shirt and leather sandals asked him for a dollar. Calust stared at him, memorizing the man's worn face, the grey beard, the braid hanging out from beneath his red canvas cap. "You've never seen someone who needs a buck, pal?" the panhandler asked. "You don't speak English?"

Without pause, Calust continued down the sidewalk, and, at that moment, he decided to let Uncle Krikor's story become part of the inside world. He made the decision, like his father had, to not tell the story. He never told Arpi. Never told Taline. He didn't even want to tell himself. Instead, he had let it go to the dim places of his mind, to wherever the stream of subconscious might go. To wherever riptides came from.

The phone rang at six the next morning. Calust found himself disoriented. He couldn't recall having fallen asleep the night before. His calves burned from the previous day's hike.

"They found him."

"Arpi?"

"We found him, Cal. He was hiding at a friend's house."

"Friend?"

She explained that one of the police detectives assigned to their case had contacted Hal's school. From there, he'd been put in touch with teachers and students. It turned out that Hal had told some of his classmates that he'd planned to hide out at a close friend's house. The parents of the friend were out of town for the weekend. The police had arrived at dawn, woke Hal and took him home. "So he didn't run away," Calust suggested.

"Yes he did. He said that he did it to punish Ken and me."

"Arpi, boys of that age, they sometimes go wild."

"It's the divorce," she said. "I think he's troubled by it."

Calust said nothing.

"But the divorce had to happen, Cal. You know that."

"Of course," he said. "There was no choice but to leave Ken." He felt like Arpi was waiting for him to say something more, so he said, "I'm happy you found the boy."

As he walked to the shower, he considered his afternoon in the scrubby hills. He thought about his sister's family and their troubles. Ken had often ignored Arpi, and now both parents, cash-strapped by legal fees, were ignoring the boy. He regarded his naked body, age spots, wrinkles, grey hair, and even in the face of all this evidence, he still sometimes felt like a boy himself, as though he only carried the authority, the wisdom, and maturity of a sleepy child. So he turned on cold water, let it wash over him, and shivered and gasped in a way that felt good.

He went to a Denny's for breakfast and then unlocked the shop. He swept the corners and took a moment to note the lack of character- no leather chairs, no wood detail, no brass trim- and considered that maybe it was time to invest in some decoration. He dusted all three stations, although he rarely needed more than one, counted his bank, made sure he had a backstore of mousses, gels, shampoos, disinfectants, then turned on the neon sign.

Kevin Lany, a local plumber, was his first customer. "Give me a trim," he said. "How's life, Cal?"

Calust nodded. "Life," he answered. A steady trickle of customers came through until lunch, and when the store emptied out completely, he closed the door, turned up the AC, took out fishing wire and wax, and tried once more to pull off Krikor's parlor trick. Yet again, he failed. *You have left quite a legacy, Uncle*, he thought.

At first the boy was *grounded*, some American form of punishment as alien to Calust as divorce, but after a few weeks, he was allowed out again. When Calust came to pick him up, he wore hiking boots, blue jeans and a black t-shirt with a picture of guitar. Underneath, the word *Electric*. "I like your shirt," said Calust. "It is interesting, but not rude."

Hal shifted in his seat.

"Are you ready? If we are lucky, we might see the coyote."

"*The Coyote*. Will he be chasing *the Roadrunner*?"

"I don't understand."

Instead of answering, Hal stared out the window.

"Hovig?"

"Hal."

"Are you ready, Hal?"

Hal nodded.

Calust considered for a moment then started the car. "You know, you are not the only one in our family to be in trouble."

"Mom already gave me a speech," Hal said.

"Your Uncle Krikor was a morphine peddler in the underground market." And he spoke in English, as best he could, which wasn't very good, and he could see that Hal was doing his best to pretend not to care, staring out the window as they left Simi for the hills. Calust continued anyway, describing events, giving bits of details, stumbling over his vocabulary. His concern was less to impress the boy than to tell the story. He wanted to paint a picture of Krikor's movie-star smile. His father's bitter silence. The story of the kings of Armenia in their fortress of treasures. Krikor's morphine-fueled vision of the dead. A betrayal within a family. The curve and indent of guns beneath black coats. Lala Jafarian's white fingers making the sign of the cross. A small boy trying to pee, frozen under the gaze of a government hitman. Hal regarded him from the corners of jaded eyes with a well-practiced look of distrust, but that, Calust decided, was alright; there was some good to be had from all this. And Calust went on: testing his memory, pausing for breath, telling the story.

At the Bottom of the Pool, Point Dume, CA

At the Bottom of the Pool, Point Dume, CA first appeared in Ararat Quarterly.

A jug of antifreeze sloshes in Sasha's nervous hands. "Hola cat," he says to Shitball the cat who just stares up at him through the holly. Sasha will not kill Gerald's cat. He isn't the type. Or, maybe he is. If he is, it's temporary insanity, which he'll blame on one day of sexual vertigo; the day Gerald found out that he was cheating. Gerald threw him out. Now, all Sasha wants is quick absolution, some way back to love, and if Gerald won't give it, then Sasha will force the issue.

So, he's going to kill the cat. He glances past her, past the fern garden, across the pool. No one there. Sasha is all jitters and he has good reason to be- in the past week Gerald has threatened to call Roberts and Tass, the massive bouncers from the Royal Martini, down on him. Never taking his eyes off the house, he puts down a can of tuna and pours antifreeze right over the top. Pooling in dusky sunlight, it reflects like chrome. "Psst, come here Shitball," he hisses. She does not move. Her pudgy face is frozen like she's trying to remember something bad. Shitball is a fat, flat-faced Himalayan Cat and doesn't answer to anything. Her real

name, the one Gerald gave her, is "Madame Butterfly",
though she doesn't answer to that, either.

The windows at Gerald's home are all draped shut but
Sasha can still picture all the rooms inside. This is it, he tells
himself, his final act of hate. Love. Whatever. He can't
catalogue all these feelings. He's going to poison the cat,
leave town, and never think about it. But how can he leave or
even stop thinking about the things he's done? He never set
out to smash mailboxes, or stalk anyone over the phone, or
kill a cat. Not at all, but then he hasn't hurt like this in a long
time. Maybe he felt this way when his parents, possibly the
only old Armenian hippies in the known world, didn't make
high school graduation and he came home to find a note
saying they'd gone to a crystal healing hike. Attached was a
twenty dollar bill, a coupon for pizza; next to that, a pack of
cigarettes. He didn't smoke.

Sasha pushes the tuna at Shitball. Tahitian Albacore
White; it's a favorite of European chefs, if you trust the label.
With his allergies to animal dander, Sasha never liked cats,
and Shitball, in particular, became a sticky point between
Gerald and himself. Sasha would wake with red eyes and a
scratchy throat. Nothing was spared: the white leather
couches, the "foxhunt" rugs, all coated with an invisible layer
of animal skin. He had to take allergy shots. And he
complained, but Gerald refused to ban her, even during sex.
Knowing the damn thing was in the room gave Sasha a
creepy sense of performance anxiety. Where was she? Under
the bed, or maybe behind the fringed curtains. So he began

to call her Shitball. At first, privately, then in front of Gerald, and finally at black tie things. Friends and visitors split into two camps: the young Turks, Sasha's friends from places like the Royal Martini, took up Shitball, while Gerald's old college pals stuck with the standard, Madame Butterfly.

She hunches like she's going to bolt and Sasha, holding his breath, backs up a few steps. He is testing the power of his patience. Shitball, sniffing, comes out from under the holly. Some part of Sasha's body, where he imagines his appendix could be, begins to tingle. After walking around the can a few times, Shitball squishes her face into it. She chews with wet smacks, then coughs her food up onto the lawn.

This has taken far too long. "Godamn!" He snaps and throws a dirty kick at Shitball who is on her toes and, despite a lot of fat, leaping away in a blur. Somehow, he nails her, but it feels like kicking a feather, not the solid crack he wants. She falls into a frantic tumble and lands with her leg making a celery-snap sound, followed by crazy yowls.

Before Sasha can think, he sees a glass door slide open. Gerald, only in briefs and fuzzy rabbit slippers, steps out. Where the hell did he come from? The yellow kitchen broom Gerald holds means that he thinks Shitball's got into a fight with a neighbor cat, so Gerald stops when he notices Sasha. They look at each other from across the pool which Sasha wishes was much bigger. All the dogs from the neighborhood begin to bark. "Godamn Sasha! Are you crazy?" Seeing Gerald like that; belly hanging over underwear elastic, choking the plastic broom like a bat, puts an unintended grin on Sasha's face. He pictures himself running, being bopped on the head by Gerald, a chubby avenger in underwear, and then Sasha starts to giggle. "Gerald, I'm sorry."

"No." Kneeling, Gerald scoops up his cat. "I can't believe what you did. I'm gonna call the police."

Bending over to catch his weight on the diving board, Sasha laughs in hacks, a muffled laugh punctured with empty gasps. Then, Gerald hits him with the broom and it doesn't hurt and he laughs harder.

The cops don't think this is funny, though. The cuffs, too tight, bite into Sasha's wrists and his fingertips go numb. "I don't know who you think you are," says one cop when they push him through processing, "but you're sick in the head." The other cop has his hand under Sasha's armpit, digging his knuckles into the soft flesh there. Sasha keeps his head down and his long blue hair falls over his face. He wishes he hadn't asked Gerald to color it like that because men are watching him from behind bars. Some are lean and covered in tattoos and, for a second, he mistakes one for Johnny. This is a place Johnny might be.

Processing is cluttered with over-spilled files, and beat up printers that spit out paper with a sound that reminds Sasha of shredders. Dust mingles with institutional cleaning stuff, coffee, and printer ink. Finger prints, photos, computer scans; they have too many ways of making sure that he's nailed down a criminal. He can't believe he's here. This, more than anything, makes him slump when he meets the block guard, a small man wearing a mustache with pointy ends, who reminds him of Errol Flynn. "You will be put in 13-H. No one else is in there, yet." says Flynn. He is told to take a top bunk and he'd better not ruin his blanket. He shouldn't use much toilet paper as it's only replaced twice a week and that this is Lot A, which has the first cafeteria round. Be sure to be up by six or he won't eat. There's some paperwork to finish and then Sasha gets phone time. Does he want phone time?

When Sasha doesn't say anything, Flynn asks for a sign that he understands. Sasha answers with a spastic hiccup. Slits of light crawl through the windows and flare, white, across the block guard's balding head, "Nod or give me verbal acknowledgement, you stupid fuck."

As the door closes, Sasha nods.

The place is claustrophobically mashed into the corner of the cell block. He can barely stretch, and if you're sitting on the toilet, you could wash your hands at the same time. The beds are narrow and they creak. Taped above his bunk are three pictures, which he'd expect, of naked women, and also a strange photo, maybe from National Geographic, of the head of an ostrich. It's black eyeballs glare down; the slick magazine paper making them shiny. What sort of person would put up the photo of an ostrich? Did someone masturbate to it, he wonders.

An hour later, Flynn brings him to the phone. It's a disturbing thing, with hard plastic trying to be metal and a receiver that's too big for Sasha's head, but what bothers him, mostly, is that there's no coin slot. A coin slot would offer some sense of control.

The guard passes a hand over his wristwatch, "Hurry up, don't you have anyone?"

Who can he call? He doesn't have a lawyer and won't get a public one for two weeks. His parents could be anywhere in their Double Eagle mobile home and he couldn't fathom where to begin such a talk. How many years would he need to play back, or skip, dizzy, to the present and hope somehow his parents make the connection? He can't expect that, they've had so few connections before. They've always been like eccentric neighbors. Sasha's friends from home are poor and friends from LA have been stand-offish since the story went out that he slept with Johnny. People who used to buy him drinks at the Martini now give him short, dirty stares. For a moment, he thinks about calling Johnny.

"Times up," says the guard.

Each day, new men are added to the cell. They smell like old towels and remind Sasha that he must also smell. At night, the ostrich looks bigger, especially the eyes. He goes back in his life and find some reasonable moment for an ostrich and there is none. He considers birds, all kinds, and realizes he's never really looked at them. He can't even recall the blur that birds make when they flap. His senses move to a heightened awareness, and he is conscious of bars and metal. Now, all he can hear is the pained crack of the bed frame when he moves, the snores, and electric hum of security equipment.

This would have been a bad dream a year ago when he was stretched across the white couch with Gerald, making loving promises. There were so many promises. Back then, Gerald finished paying back all kinds of loans and bought a home at Point Dume at Malibu with the cash windfall from Hair Sushi. For a moment, they both lived in Gerald's life, like the year round cacti on the hills behind their home. Sometimes, Sasha could drag Gerald out to Rage or the Martini, but found himself seeing more of Gerald's friends, drinking lattes on the back porch. Nights, they cooked together. Gerald bought a stainless steel oven with six burners. They made fried shrimp chips, tomato and carrot-cheddar stew, black and white ice baby-cakes. Once, Sasha stood over the sink, snapping snow peas, dropping them into an oak bowl. The crack-crack sound was a friendly rhythm. He glanced up through a sky window and saw thunderhead clouds smashed between the horizon and the edge of outer space. With trade winds picking up, he could smell salt water through the patio door. He let cool air go down his throat, then put the peas down and looked at Gerald, who was slicing red onions. Gerald smiled liked Buddha and Sasha felt a touch of guilt, but he didn't know why, yet.

That year, Sasha wore denim shorts and traded them for khakis at night. He rode horses or looked on the beach for blue shells, watched football and men and PBS specials on windsurfing or tropical birds. They slept close together; he liked Gerald's soft hair against his lips and, sometimes, let the ends fall in his mouth where he would roll them between his tongue and lips, and he wondered if the trade winds that hung outside came from anywhere exotic or if they were going there. He got a job offer from one of Gerald's long-time customers. "Information disposal tech," he was told.

"What?" he asked.

He traveled to offices with a paper shredder, and a *demagnitizer* trying to guess what kind of secrets were so big that people would pay to have them erased. He bought a Saturn, joined the Bulldog Gym, and since he was Downtown after his route, found himself coming back to the Royal Martini. There, he could drink and idle and not have to think about a creepy confusion that was shadowing him. He was not used to stability. He'd grown up in the shaky world of his parents, very young people with unchecked energy, but not any energy they wanted to focus- his father playing atari while smoking pot in the kitchen, his mother reading tarot for Deadhead friends. They smoked a lot. He wondered if the old myth was true that the children of smokers are born impatient and unstable.

Sometimes, they would just get in their Double Eagle RV and leave him with one of a bunch of aunts or uncles, none of whom, he was later to learn, were related to him. Thinking about them, he might only recall nicknames: the TV uncle, the aunt with the parrots. Some had chores for him; or sent him to school. One took him to woods to pick mushrooms, and his favorite uncle would bring him to a disco and leave him up in the DJ's crow's nest. Below, light burst off the rim of a huge disco ball. After, Sasha's parents would show up and take him back. Sometimes, he would play a game in which he could, through sheer will, become invisible and walk through walls like a ghost so he could slip into the RV and go with them.

Getting home late once- after he'd been with Gerald a little more than a year, Sasha paced the backyard. He took off his shoes and waded into the pool, and let the cold leak into his legs, up to his groin. He found himself face to face with a giant pool toy, a blow up rubber duck. "So Dorothy," he told it, "so you got over that rainbow, but then you were all hot to get home, weren't you?" The duck didn't look the right color in moonlight. In bed, he was sure, Gerald's body was warm.

"Where were you?" said Gerald, sliding over.

"Nowhere."

"Your feet are freezing!" Gerald yelped as Sasha looked for Shitball.

Sometimes, Gerald went on trips, hair shows, and Sasha didn't mind this as he knew Gerald, the victim of an affair once before, was doggedly monogamous. Sasha would rent a few movies, lock Shitball out, and watch them on the big screen. Or sometimes, put on tight blue jeans, glossy boots, and a white shirt that showed his nipples and drive to the Martini. He saw pals or ex-lovers, and they teased him about settling down. "You don't get it," he told them, "Gerald is a nice guy."

And Gerald was a nice guy. Sasha had felt that on his first trip to Hair Sushi. He'd just broke up with a life guard from Long Beach, and, out of a distilled sense of frustration, decided to treat himself to a two hundred dollar change in hair style. He heard good things about Sushi, and Gerald. Walking through the narrow galley there Sasha found himself surrounded by a series of scents: aloe, alcohol, mint, dye, papaya, bleach, peach, make-up remover, avocado. Somehow, he thought he could smell the steel that scissors were made from.

"What shade?" was the was the first thing Gerald asked.

"Sky blue. Sky."

"When I'm finished," said Gerald, "they wont be able to tell where your head ends and where the air begins."

"That's not funny." but it was, and then, grinning, Sasha began his usual story of hair complaints; dry scalp, the cowlick over his left ear, having to choose between long and short. Nodding, Gerald suggested a citrus based treatment and explained how the smog was no good for anyone, especially dry scalps.

"Well, it's better than the earthquakes," Sasha smiled.

They got on to disaster movies, and settled on *Titanic* as their favorite. "It was the acting," Gerald said, "the people who were able to make love seem important again."

"That's my love life, Gerald. It's a disaster."

"Yeah?"

"I just broke up with my guy. He was a player, I never could get a straight answer out of him."

Gerald guided the back of Sasha's head into a bowl of lime-scented conditioner, asking if the Life Guard was a party boy. Of course he was a party boy. If he'd been an action figure, he would have come with his own tiny, plastic bong and bottle of tequila. Everyone Sasha knew was a party boy, and he was sure these people had all rubbed off on him the wrong way. Gerald wrinkled his forehead with a little protest.

"You know," Sasha said, "How, if you know people for a while, they start to expect you to act a certain way and then you act that way. Not because you want to, but because they won't let you be another way."

"I don't know, Sasha, you have to just be the way you are."

"No, no. You can't change in the face of all that expectation."

"That's like something a Freudian-cum-Calvinist would say."

"A what?"

"Oh, it doesn't mean a thing, it's a joke from my grad days."

It hadn't occurred to Sasha that a hair dresser would have a PhD in anything and he found himself unevenly divided between intimidated, and interested. He ran through the conversation they'd just had, hoping he hadn't said anything stupid. Finally he said, "I want it blue. Can you make my hair a good blue?"

"Yeah," said Gerald. Sasha felt his hair was a weighty thing in Gerald's hands. Gerald's own head was covered in a thinning widow's peak, a touch of mellow-handed maturity that gave people the sense that he had reached his age with what people call "substance". This was counter-pointed by his eyes, in which Sasha could discern a childlike capacity for innocence or something like that.

There was a small group of people with bad hair who called Gerald a philosopher. Old friends from UCLA. They'd meet and drink lattes. Hair Sushi wasn't mentioned much in this company, and most of them referred to it only as "Gerald's work". "I met him at work," Gerald would say about Sasha. There was a Paris feeling to those nights and Sasha accepted them as part of Gerald's universe and, later, it all made him feel better about his solo junkets to the Martini.

The Martini was where he met slick characters or roughnecks. There, he'd met Roberts and Tass, two big, Lithuanian bouncers. He also met Johnny. Johnny was like a villain from an old B movie, riding some chromed-out Harley. He hung out with men who did not dance or flirt. They were on the down-low. Pierced and tatted, they huddled in corners where the light would barely go. Sasha couldn't imagine that they had homes to go to. They probably spent their lives on motorcycles, in other peoples' beds, in cheap hotels in Tijuana or Vegas.

They met on one of the weekends that Gerald was away. Just a quick introduction, and he didn't think about it again until much later. By then, he was drunk and didn't want to go back to an empty house and face the cat and overdue videos. Instead, he found a party in some Hollywood hole in a wall where one of the walls, being redone, was covered by a giant blue tarp. Johnny was there. They talked, a flickering conversation Sasha couldn't recall the next morning. They stood by the punch and Sasha drank and drank even after someone accidentally dropped a rusty set of keys into the bowl. "You wanna ride my Harley?" Johnny finally said.

At the door, they brushed by Tass. "Nuts to you, my friend," he said to Sasha, dropping the words in a thick Slavic chuckle. That's what Tass said to everyone. It was his hello and his goodbye. Drunk in possibilities, Sasha shot him a dirty glance and walked out, one hand around Johnny's bony wrist. Everyone saw them go together.

The noise of the engine bled through Sasha's groin, up his spine, and into his temples. Johnny's leather jacket kept Sasha's chest warm and through it, he felt gliding muscles. The tip of his penis pushed against the back of his fly. North of Glendale, they passed a small field of blinking lights. "Fairies!" Sasha yelled.

Johnny pulled over. "What?"

"Fairies. In Ireland, they have bog fairies and they shine lights to trick people, so they get lost. They have a really long name for them. I don't remember, but it's funny."

"It's just a carnival," said Johnny.

"Let's go."

"It's closed," but Johnny rumbled the cycle down to a park. Someone had left the lights on but everything else, the ferris wheel, the rocket-spinner, the fun house hunched like old monuments. The red light on the carousel winked and then burned out. Holding his breath, Sasha brought his face close to Johnny's. They came together over a rough kiss. "There's the fun house," Johnny pointed. Then, he put the end of his finger between Sasha's lips and Sasha took a soft bite. "Let's go. Let's have fun."

I'm drunk, thought Sasha when they squeezed under the fence, passed a teenaged night watchman who was stoned asleep below the carousel, and made a run to the funhouse. Clutching the spare motorcycle helmet, Sasha felt like Indiana Jones. The earth beneath his feet was a spinning, dirty paradise. "I always wanted to fuck in the funhouse!" Johnny told him.

"I was always wanted to, too," said Sasha but he meant always as in "right now". Right now had the potency of always. It was a shitty funhouse, like someone added wings to an outhouse, but there were mirrors. Fat and skinny, upside down and right side up, flesh bobulating or stretching like taffy, they fucked in every room and Sasha felt Johnny's penis glowing like a light in his body.

A little before sun up, they reached Johnny's apartment. There were racks of guns, monkey boots, gas masks, and army gear all over the walls. "Jesus- Johnny, are you one of those militia men?"

"No," Johnny nodded at all the stuff, "it's my roommate's."

"Wow." They barely made it to the bed. "Will O' the Wisp," Sasha said with a dizzy nod in Johnny's direction. But Johnny was crashed, snoring. "Those Irish fairies, Johnny, they're called Will O' the Wisp. They trick people." he said anyway.

When he woke, he stared at Johnny's body which reminded him of worn jeans: small ripples of scars, faded tattoos, and there were no sags, but hollow spots instead. In the daylight, the dark skin around Johnny's eyes became obvious. Sasha felt woozy and unsure. He let Johnny sleep, ambled into the living room, and met Johnny's roommate, a man with big, square shoulders, who wouldn't give his name but said everybody called him Badger. Badger invited him to watch *Lucy* on the tiny TV stuck under a rack of camouflage helmets, and then gave Sasha some rice puff cereal. "So, how is it living with Johnny?" Sasha finally asked.

"S'okay," Badger said, "he's ok, but he's a slob. I'm letting him stay as a favor to a friend. "Howsit sleeping with him?"

Sasha took another spoonful of cereal.

"Never mind," said Badger, "It's just that I wouldn't trust him."

Sasha didn't see Badger as the type to be jealous and so he guessed that Badger was simply unaware of the raw sex that pumped through his roommate who snored until noon, got up, scratched his balls and asked for a blow job. Sasha said he didn't feel like it and Johnny cursed. And when Badger, never taking his eyes off *Lucy*, told him to shut up, Johnny switched to begging for sex.

"I have to go. I have to go." said Sasha.

"OK, let me drive you."

"No, it's OK, I'll take the bus." But Sasha couldn't find a bus stop; he called a cab to bring him back to his Saturn that was covered in parking tickets. Going back to Malibu, he felt like he was breathing funny. He thought of divers who rise too fast. The bends, they call it the bends. He had a mad idea that, if he got home in time- to the pool, there were these blue shadows at the deep end he could hide in. His hands were sweaty.

The next day, Gerald came home and Sasha pretended to be napping so he wouldn't have to go down and say *hi*, but it didn't help because he knew that Gerald knew. They sat at dinner with red potatoes, red salad and wine, and Gerald answered Sasha's questions about Dallas with nods. The food sat wrong. "I'm tired," Gerald said not touching the dessert, "I'm so tired I'm going to go to sleep." In bed, when Sasha slid a meek arm around Gerald's waist, Gerald let it stay but didn't touch Sasha back.

And when Sasha got back late from work the next day, he found all the glass doors draped shut. "It's OK," he talked to himself. The pool was covered, the doors locked, and locks had been changed. Impossible. He walked around the yard. Even Shitball was gone. He cursed through the windows. "It was a fling!" This was impossible. He hadn't realized how quickly Gerald's money could move things. The moment seemed cartoonish and staged. If he wasn't frightened by his acceptance of being locked out of his own home, he might have laughed. He drove to a pay phone. "Hi this is Gerald," said the answering machine, "I'll be gone a few weeks..."

Sasha took a room at a hotel and called every day. He lagged at work and found himself angry at the idea of waking early and shaving. He called mutual friends trying to find out where Gerald was, but they played stupid and even after he came back from Tahiti or where-ever, Gerald changed his number and Sasha resorted to dialing up Hair Sushi, tying up the lines. Sasha showed up at work with a terrible hangover and he was told, maybe, it was time to leave.

He moved to a small place in Van Nuys and every morning he would call his credit card company to find out exactly how little money he had left. Sometimes, he would stare at his reflection in the mirror and watch the black roots cropping out under his azure hair. He tried to imagine what his mind felt like trapped in that pale head and he had the sensation that he was looking at someone entirely different from himself, someone whom he'd only accidentally been caught up in affairs with. He went back to Malibu, climbed the gate, rang the bell eleven times- he counted. Leaving the chain on, Gerald opened the door a crack. An eye was all Sasha could see.

"Yeah." said Gerald.

"Hey, let me in."

"I can't."

"Godamn it! I love you, you dumb fuck!" The door shut. Sasha screamed all sorts of emotional things, things he found amazing. Many were lies, but he did want forgiveness, even if he couldn't quite come out and ask for it, that's what he was there for.

The door opened, all the way this time. "I'm sorry," said Gerald, He said he couldn't trust Sasha anymore, not all the way. "You're younger and have more... life." Sasha was going to say something. "Don't interrupt. Please, this is impossible to talk about; this whole relationship has to end. Send me your new address and I'll mail you your stuff. Because I don't have time. I'm too old to be screwed by the same person twice. OK? OK." Gerald spoke with resolve, like that was it and that was all.

Sasha reached out to hug him and Gerald hurled the door shut. Sasha kicked it and it creaked under the blows. Gerald yelled from the other side for him to go away. If he didn't, he would call the police; he would call Tass and Roberts.

Sasha spit and took fast strides back to his car. He let his embarrassment distill and two days later, came back with a baseball bat and smashed Gerald's mail box. He wasn't quite sure why he did it, like in a dream. Then he drove to West Hollywood and put steel nails into the tires on Gerald's Benz. He didn't know how he was able to get back home, but he woke later with a stomach cramp and he remembered Shitball. *I'm going to kill that cat*, he thought.

Near dawn, his sixth day in holding, the ostrich watches Sasha, and he can't sleep. He reaches up and rips the picture from the wall, tucks it into the back of his shorts, and paces.

The man in the bunk below snores. Sasha needs to get out, and the moment breakfast begins, he finds Flynn and demands to use the phone. He calls Johnny, but Badger answers instead and starts to say that he's not a referral service.

"Look, I'm in jail."

There is hesitation, then Badger gives him a number. "I kicked Johnny out when he threw a half a dozen forks in the disposal."

Late, around nine, he gets Johnny and begins to talk. At first, he only hears telephone static from the other end, then Johnny takes a long drag of something. A Cigar? "Over a cat?" Johnny asks him, "I thought you hate cats."

"I do."

"Are you crazy? How much is bail?"

"I need eight hundred to get out. I need it Johnny."

Johnny says he'll see.

"What about the money?" Sasha says again.

"It's all I can do Sasha. I gotta go."

"I'll do anything," Sasha says to the dial tone. It occurs to him that Gerald must also be somewhere. On a phone. Talking to the brothers, Tass and Roberts. Gerald wouldn't have thought to do it right away. Gerald has been avoiding this, hoping things would die down. First, he'll take Shitball to the vets, get an update on the leg, then go home, scratch his head and try to reconcile all his notions of the good and bad of people and try to find a place on that scale for Sasha. Then, he'll call the brothers.

Tass is the one with the mobile phone, "Nuts to you," he says. Gerald explains the situation. He's open about it. He chokes up when it comes to talking about the affair, and about Shitball, but he doesn't lie. Never blinking, Tass gives occasional grunts; "I knew that guy was shit, when we saw him with Johnny."

Can they do something? A restraining order means nothing in this town. Tass says something about we'll see and makes suggestions that Sasha doesn't want to think about. Gerald says no, no violence. He does not espouse violence, but he has eyes. Almost red now, he rubs them. He watches the TV; hears a throbbing eggbeater sound, a police helicopter, buzzing the hills. Gerald thinks of his cat's broken leg. "Unless, necessary. No violence unless absolutely necessary."

"We'll do this for you, buddy," says Tass, joining his brother back at the corner of the bar, both looking constrained by their Argentinean suits. They will do this for him, but not because Gerald is close. Just like everybody, he's scared of them; they'll do this because they think Sasha is a little, sneering punk who should be taught a lesson.

Sasha knows it could be better to stay in jail.

He knows it's Johnny two days later when Flynn opens the door. "You got bailed," Flynn says.

Johnny is waiting outside the station. Slouching in dark shades, he stares at the sidewalk. Sasha kisses him. "Are you crazy? There's cops everywhere." Almost brutally, Johnny hustles him into a car.

"I knew you'd come."

"You're lucky, a deal came through for me." Johnny lights up. "But you gotta help me do a run."

Sasha looks at the streets of LA splashing by and can't hold back a shiver. Even with the smog, the sky burns dizzy funhouse blue. Fuck. Anything, he'll do anything. "Where did you get the car?"

"I borrowed it. We're gonna need it. Tonight."

"A sale?"

"Yeah, we gotta meet some bad boys at ten."

Johnny's new place is a little better furnished than jail. "It's not really mine," he confesses. Sasha finds an inflatable mattress, and Johnny tells him there's a pump for it somewhere. They don't sleep together, Johnny's too busy with plans, mumbling over the phone, but Sasha doesn't care- he lets his mind go, feels free to throw his arms out from the center of his body. He's not sure how long he sleeps before Johnny, whose eyes have become red, shakes him, "Come on."

"Coffee?"

"No time." Then Johnny shoots off to the kitchen, "No, I'll get you some." He makes terrible instant coffee and Sasha gets through half a cup before they go.

They drive to West Hollywood, and Sasha immediately recognizes the alley behind the Royal Martini. "Isn't it a little public?"

Johnny gets out, slams the door. "Help me with some bags. They're in the trunk."

As Sasha gets out, a huge form shoves him, pins him against the side of the car. "Nuts to you, my friend."

Sasha's loud curses are cut off by the sucking pain of a punch thrown into his lower gut, and Johnny mumbles an apology as he's paid off by Roberts, "It was you or me, Sasha." They give him a thousand dollars. Sasha moans; if Johnny needs to apologize, then its going to be bad. There is a room under the Martini, filled with pipes and hard ceramic things. Over here, they beat him, punch him in the stomach until Sasha feels like he's swallowed glass, kick his shins, bitch-slap him. Sasha's feet slide around under him and then he passes out.

When he wakes, there is a third face looking down on him, very familiar but too fuzzy to make out. Sasha can't open his right eye.

"There he is, G-man." says Tass.

Gerald's face comes into blurred focus. Can Gerald see the pain on Sasha's face? Is there blood? He feels heat. He feels like he's swallowed the Rock of Gibraltar with its sharp crags. Biting through the gag, he tries to tell Gerald to leave. He doesn't want to be seen like this. Roberts and Tass look like sweaty buffalo with their shirts off.

"What did you do? *Fucking God*, get him to a hospital."

"Relax," says Tass, "he'll live just fine."

Roberts grunts his approval.

They won't let Gerald take him to a hospital, because it would be reported to the police. So Sasha is moved to a private practice in Simi Valley, way out in the suburbs. A doctor, a tanned, handsome older man, tends to him silently and efficiently. For some reason, the walls covered with motivational posters. "Strive for excellence" says one.

He hears Gerald's voice saying, "I didn't know he had an ulcer."

"He had one building up, a nasty hole on the upper left side, and the... fall ruptured it, " says the Doctor. "He should have had this checked earlier, but he'll get through it."

"I didn't know he had an ulcer." Gerald says over and over.

They give him drugs and the days get to be like colored streaks; different people, specialists maybe, go in and out, touching Sasha's naked body like it's his funeral with all these strangers come to pay respects and he wonders if any of these are his forgotten "aunts" or "uncles". Or maybe his parents came by and he didn't quite notice.

It turns out the Doctor's name is Higgenbotham.

"Is that German?" Sasha asks on one if his better days.

"Dutch," says Higgenbotham as he fills in some paperwork. "Just Dutch."

Sasha considers making some lame *Nazi joke*- this doctor is so cool and efficient in his white coat- but he thinks better of possibly antagonizing the man.

"You're all right," says Gerald, "I dropped charges on you. You can stay here til' your good enough to do whatever."

"Here? Where's that?" Sasha demands.

"You're in my house, Sasha. The upstairs den."

"The upstairs den doesn't have a bed."

"I took the desk out and put a bed in."

"Oh," Sasha raises his head slightly, "Hey, is Shitball here?"

"Yeah. Call me when you're hungry," says Gerald before closing the door. Shitball wanders the house, limping with a tiny kitty-cast for her leg. Sometimes, she stares at Sasha but won't go into his room. When Sasha is able to get around, she doesn't let him closer than ten steps. At first, he uses a walker, then cane, and finally is on his feet, but his steps are quiet, tentative. His stay must last for weeks but he isn't sure how to track time as each day is sunny and windy and sandy like the one before.

Sometimes, Gerald is distant. He stands outside the room and stares like he's never seen this creature before, wondering why he let Sasha in. But more and more, he becomes motherly, sometimes reading to Sasha, cooking for him, able to reach out now because Sasha is no longer any threat. Sasha can barely lift a soup spoon to his mouth without shaking. Sasha promises to move out but Gerald insists there is no hurry. "Wait for the symptoms to fade," he says. And they do fade, but are replaced by others. He starts to vomit. After the stomach cramps pass, his left ear hurts, then his temples. When the headaches clear, he wakes with red eyes; he becomes lethargic. He watches TV; eats. Watches TV. Sleeps. He pretends to have more headaches so he doesn't have to get up.

He's lost; his misery gets big, too massive for the room. It spreads across the house, pushing furniture out of the way, scaring Shitball, threatening to collapse the walls. He wonders if it will grow so big that he might turn into a whale and slip into the ocean. "Or an ostrich," he tells Shitball, "I'll stick my head six feet under." He laughs at that, tucking his knees together under the blankets. Looking at the cat, he feels some kinship. They've both been beat down, both on the mend. He offers his hand. She sniffs the air near him. "You gonna be my friend, girlfriend?" She just stares. He looks at the clock. Five-thirty AM. "Don't worry, baby," he tells her, "we'll be out of here, soon." He shuffles to the mirror. Of course, his swollen eyes are healed but now there are hollow crinkles all around them. His cheeks and jaw are white and puffy. and his hair stands up at crazy angles like a black and blue dandelion. With no idea of where to go, he is full of feelings of leaving. But instead, all he has to do is go across the hall, and open Gerald's door. Automatically, Gerald sits up, covering his chest with sheets. "Gerald, I'm sick, man. You gotta cut my hair."

"What time is it?" Gerald slides on reading glasses. "It's five-thirty. Are you crazy?"

"You always ask me that. I have to get a hair cut."

Gerald snorts and shakes his head.

"Then I'm going to leave."

"You're in no shape."

Sasha wants to scream, to kick furniture, at least slam the door, but holds still instead. He is testing the powers of his patience. "I'm gonna cry, Gerald."

"It's five-thirty."

"I'll still cry, anyway."

They wheel an office chair to the side of the pool. Water catches the first few slips of sunlight. Gerald starts to cut. Sasha finds the sliding-snip noise calming. Not something he would listen for or even think about, but a reassuring sound of something being done that you can't take back. By looking down, he can see his shadow in the water. There, wind creates ripples and his shadow vanishes and returns, each time with a little less hair. Feathery bundles of blue-tipped black hair drift into the pool.

"This has to end, Gerald. But when? When can I go?"

"When you're better." Gerald stops cutting for a moment and brushes clipped ends off Sasha's collar, "When you're better. I don't know."

Again, they're quiet. Sasha waits until his sideburns are clean and they hug his face before he talks again, "Gerald, there's a question I have for you."

"Yeah?"

"Why do I feel like a ghost?"

"What."

"A ghost," says Sasha. "No, not a ghost. When I was a kid I used to pretend I was a ghost and that was okay. I'm something that's not okay; I'm just uprooted, Gerald. I can tell you all the places I've been but nothing I've said or done at those places seems to mean anything right now. Isn't it going to be the same about right now? Will any of this matter nine months from now?"

"Maybe."

"No."

"You're just tired, Sasha. You'll feel better later." Gerald switches to a smaller scissor and brush. "Don't move," he warns, as he clips close to Sasha's skin.

"You know how you went to grad school and got that PhD in Philosophy? Doesn't it ever bug you that you make a living as a barber?"

"It doesn't matter about what I'm better at. Philosophy is the art of bringing ourselves to a higher mind. It's noble."

"If that's philosophy, and I'll believe you, then what's a haircut, Gerald? I mean, if philosophy brings us to a higher mind, then what do haircuts do?" Sasha is careful to hold onto the chair now. He feels light headed and his head shakes. Gerald's hand, for the first time ever, slips. A few fat drops of blood run down Sasha's ear. He feels their heat in his ear canal. Several apologies later, Gerald covers it with a think bandage and finishes quickly.

A tiny electric trimmer finishes off the edges of Sasha's eyebrows. "Sometimes a haircut is just a haircut." says Gerald.

"But sometimes not," says Sasha. Gerald wrinkles his forehead as if to say, cut the crap, man. Sasha hunches forward so he can stare at his reflection, "I don't know, but it's beautiful, Gerald, it's beautiful."

Gerald sighs, massages his neck and goes to make breakfast. Snoozing in his room, Sasha can smell eggs frying and english muffins toasting. The door slams; Gerald always leaves by seven. After the car rolls out the driveway, Sasha gets out of bed. He hunts up pants, a belt and big, white shirt. His energy races in front of him, burning a clean path out the front door. He hasn't been past that door in six weeks and just before it, he stops. The moment he's outside, he knows, he's on his own. No friends, no job, not a damn toothbrush. Shitball, he spots her. He guesses maybe cats have some wanderlust, "Hey Shitball, come here." Her face explodes in a goggle-eyed, fearful look and she runs, but how far can a gimpy cat go? He follows the clip-clop across foxhunt rugs, past the chrome stove, under the spilling luminescence of sky lights, and finally corners her. "It's OK, Shitball, I'm not gonna hurt you." The cat freezes like rigor mortis setting in, doubles her weight. He grabs her and, straining, lifts, tucks her under his arm like a loaf of bread. She pisses all over him.

He stares at the yellow stains. "Well, fuck. Well fuck. I suppose I deserve that. Look," he begins to walk out, grabs a towel "I'm gonna get you out of here. We can't stay here anymore. Gerald needs to find that space for someone who loves him. Really, I mean, really really. God knows, I suck at love."

He holds her so they're face to face, "You're a Himalayan Cat, right? The Himalayas? Aren't they supposed to be this great place? You don't look like you deserve that name. Neither do I. I can't let us stay in Malibu and get fat or, in your case, fatter." He walks out the door. They will travel the world and buy motorcycles. Well, Shitball can sit in a sidecar. They'll get lean, and find those Buddhist guys that hang out on mountains and give answers in the form of questions. They'll find buried gold. Then, when they have black belts and golden crowns, they'll come back. "We'll come back, right Shitball? Sorry, Madame Butterfly. We'll tell Gerald that we're sorry. And we can be friends and love him, like holy love. Right?"

The cat in his trembling arms, he steps past the driveway, and onto the road with every intention of mercy. "Come on, answer me. Animals can speak in the voice of God, or something, right? I saw it on a Christmas special." *Oh please God*, he's thinking, give me some guidelines, let the cat tell me I'm doing the right thing. Let me not smell like piss. He's walks a block and is tired. He sets her down and she waddles, peg-leg, back home. "Sorry!" he calls after her. Then, "I'm talking to a cat."

He goes back to the house, lets her in. Then, following her with his eyes, realizes how lucky, in the strangest way, he is to have Gerald. He will not travel to the ends of the earth. He will not vanish. He will go inside, sit down, and wait like a civilized human. He will ask Gerald for some advice or ideas. The two of them have reached some equilibrium where they can start again. Not as lovers, but as something. There is a future in which Sasha cannot be invisible or walk through walls. He follows the cat which is less than six feet away from him and, probably for no reason other than the fact that she feels danger has passed, but maybe not, she purrs.

Clean

Clean first appeared in The Journal.

-This is now

New shoes which are not Nike but black business shoes. A clean, white shirt with a tight collar and a tie that my father- he's almost smiling- has to help me put on. Khaki pants. I am applying for a job as a gym trainer. I can start at four hundred cash per week. From now on it's work full time and college classes at night for me. Considering how shit went down for Joker aka Abo Tavidagian on that fucked Saturday night, things have to change.

Armenians are dark and hairy people. I've had my beard since I finished high school. Now, the black hairs are falling into the bathroom sink. Shaving off the last of the stubble stings, especially under my chin, but a good kind of sting. With the beard gone, I look like a nice, hard working boy. I am taking ADD pills again. Life is becoming a solvable puzzle again; each piece goes into it directly and correctly.

Raff, my little brother, comes into my room and stands around, watches me fix my collar. "Armen, you look younger."

"Don't call me Armen."

"Armen!"

"Fuck! You better call me Poet."

"Are you going to say your name is Poet at the interview?"

"No, I need the job. Fuck off," but I say that in a joke kind of way. I smile at him in the mirror. Raff can get spooky sometimes, so I'm glad we're talking at all. Pull at my tie one more time. I tell him: "You know the right thing to do is to go to school and work hard. You don't want to end up dead or in the gutter."

He just looks at me.

-This was long ago, high school

In class, I talk too much and Abo runs provocation at me. He flicks me off or makes stupid faces so I have to say something. Sometimes he makes me laugh so hard that I think I'm going to piss myself. For example: "Tiki."

One day at lunch he says, "Tiki means pussy. Every time I say Tiki, you have to think about pussy."

"Fuck that."

"Tiki."

"Tiki doesn't mean anything Abo, it's just some bullshit word."

"Tiki."

Now he says it in class, real quiet so only I can hear. "Tiki," like a little mouse talking, and I bust up laughing, then the teacher sends me to the assistant principal's office. Abo waves goodbye as I go, and I flick him off which just serves me more trouble. He's like my second brother.

I've known Abo since forever, beginning when he tried to bite me at summer school, and he always plays the class clown. He looks the part too, short with kinky hair and a big forehead. Even my too quiet father says, "Your friend- he looks like his ancestors were scared by a dinosaur." So he had to become the class clown and be fearless, otherwise he would get his ass kicked.

As for me, I like to be entertained. To find things that fill up my head real fast. If I don't get entertained, then I feel like the walls are closing in. I feel like the lights are about to go black.

Every person has to have one friend they can say anything to. Abo is mine. We talk about girls, about girls' asses. We talk about how we wish we were black so we could rap, or how Mexican gangs are taking over the schoolyard. One day, I confess to Abo about this girl that I liked in junior high, and that I wrote a poem to her. This is how tight we are.

He's like: "No shit? I remember in grade school you liked to read poetry books."

"The girl was Emma Norsigian. You remember her?"

"Real skinny, yeah."

I say how Emma took that poem and put it in her locker so that it would show every time she opened the door. She even sent it to the school writing contest, and it won second prize.

"You're lying. I never saw you with that girl."

"That's the fucked up thing. She loved the poem, but she didn't like me. She could hardly even look at me."

"Well I don't blame her. You remember how many zits you had on your head? That's what you get for writing poems."

That's the funny kind of motherfucker Abo can be, funny enough to get me sent to the assistant principal's office.

Let me say now that I might get in trouble but am not stupid. I once read a 500 page horror novel by Clive Barker; I got an "A" in art class; I know the meaning of big words like "perturbed", "provocation" and "genocide"; and I know *To be or not to be* is from Shakespeare. I am not stupid. It's only that I have too many thought in my head.

My brain has been doing this since sixth grade, so finally the assistant principal tells me, if I don't agree to ADD pills, I could be moved to La Brea Technical. La Brea Technical is a school for retards.

My father works at his store seven days, 14 hours a day, open to close. That's why when there's trouble, it's my mother who comes to school. She works at the store too, but more normal hours, mostly eight to four.

My mother tries to tell the assistant principal that I don't need pills. Her English is bad, and she always says "Yes-no." "My son, he will not need the therapy. Yes-no, my son, he is a good boy." I try to tell her that *yes-no* doesn't mean anything; she says it anyway.

The assistant principal keeps his face the same way, all tight ass, through the whole things and says we have to sign the pill papers, and my mother never wants anybody to be angry; she fills in the forms. "Yes-no," she says one last time. If it was my father, he wouldn't say a word, but he'd be raging on the inside because to old school Armenians, saying that your son needs drugs is the same as saying: you have failed in your duty to make a healthy son. So, my mother and I decide to keep this secret from my father. I plan to keep the pills in my locker at school, but you can't have them in your locker. The school nurse holds them, and you go to her right after the lunch bell.

The pills make me quiet. I don't talk as much during class. It's like when you do a jigsaw puzzle and get those first few pieces, and suddenly the whole thing makes sense, and you just know what goes where- it fits directly and correctly. Then you sit back and kind of see the puzzle finish itself.

When I tell Abo this, he starts to dig through my backpack. "I want some," he says.

"Well, go ask the fucking assistant principal. You're the punk who always gets me in trouble, you should be taking those pills, not me."

"At least I'm not a fucking 'tard case." He pretends to be a monkey.

I hit him, and we have our only real fight. The kind of fight where your shirt gets ripped and your baggy jeans are sliding down your ass, but you don't care. I'm bigger, like I said, but he fights dirty. He bites my shoulder.

Some older Armenian boys come around and watch us like watching a dog fight. They are in a gang called Armenian Power, AP for short or sometimes known as Hye Deghak which translates to Armenian Boys. The biggest of those boys is Raider, whose real name is Greg Tavidagian- but he would beat you if you called him that. He is also Abo's second cousin and known for keeping a gun in his black Ford Bronco. I'm afraid that Raider's going to step in and kick my ass, but he just watches and nods a little.

After that, Raider tells us to hang out with him. This includes sitting at the AP table at lunch. That there is an Armenian gang in LA might surprise some people, but it's true. Armenians have had gangs since we were attacked in Turkey, but in California, the new enemies are the Mexican gangs aka cholos. There have been fights with the cholos because we are accused of stealing their style: cars, gear and music. But to this Raider says: "Fuck the beaners. The AP wore Kings and Raiders hats going way back. And it wasn't the Mexicans who invented rap but the blacks."

To add insult to injury, people think that Armenians are Mexicans because we have big noses, tan skin and tight hair. To have an enemy is bad enough without being mistaken for him.

"You should join AP," says Macaroni, a fat guy whose real name is Mike.

"Fuck that," I tell him.

Macaroni is like: "You want me to step on your neck little man?" But he doesn't do anything because the truth is he's not really a fighter.

"You'll want to join soon enough," says Raider.

"Could be," I say. But the truth is I'm not interested in AP. Maybe it's the pills, but there's no place for that shit in my jigsaw puzzle.

Abo, who is still riding the vapors of our fight, says he wants to join. Doing daredevil shit like that is in his character, like I said.

His initiation is the next day after school. Joining Armenian Power is not hardcore like some gangs you've heard of. You don't do a drive-by. And it's not like La M where you cover your body in tats. All you have to do is fight somebody for one minute. Abo chooses to fight Raider which seems like a stupid idea unless he figures Raider, being a second cousin, will take him down easy. This is a mistake. Raider throws Abo to the ground and beats him for the full sixty seconds. Abo slowly stands, covered in cuts and bruises and laughing hard, so they decide his tag will be Joker like the crazy, laughing enemy of Batman.

After he joins, Abo aka Joker wants us to spend all our time with Raider. "Just cause you're Hye Deghak doesn't mean you have to be Raider's bitch," I tell him.

But to Joker, Raider is the final solution mackdaddy, and I can see why. Raider's family lives in the hills of Glendale with a big screen TV and two growling Dobermans out back. He lets us ride in his bronco with the only rule being: don't touch the gun, but you can see the handle, a shiny chromed out piece, jammed in the crack between the front seats.

Actually, Raider isn't so bad once you get past his status of being a scary motherfucker. He gives his friends rides, beer and money without thinking twice. Almost every day, he plays video hockey, drinks corona, reads about car stereo systems and cruises Foothill Boulevard; he is a creature of habit.

But being habitual is also his flaw. He's afraid of the unknown. Here's a guy who can kick your ass, but he won't go see a horror movie. He won't drive to Long Beach because he's afraid of getting lost. He won't drive to Valencia because he almost got into an accident there. He can't stand surprises.

As time passes, Raider and I become friends anyway because, in the final breakdown, your friends are the people who sit in a car with you and drive around the city, looking out the window for I don't know what.

-After high school

I do get good grades, mostly B's. I get into Pasadena City College and then stop taking those ADD pills. Things suddenly start to move quick again. I don't know how to tell you; I feel like I must be on drugs which is funny because I'm off drugs.

My brain is reopened for mad business. I think about girls' tits. About pussy with curly black hair. I think about nintendo and subwoofers. I think about Polo, Hilfiger and

FUBU. About Reservoir Dogs and Stephen King's *Dark Tower* books. About Snoop Dogg, Bone Thugs, Onyx, Tupac and of course NWA. Bad boys with guns. I think about the sun and the heat it pours down on Van Nuys. I think about Raider's home in the hills where the wind stays cool. The pistol he carries in that bronco. Chrome. I think about cash and what it gets you.

I think about all these things at the same time. The only thing I can't think of is myself. I am nowhere to be seen. With the graduation money from my relatives I have enough to get a nintendo and some games. My days start around noon when I get my ass out of bed. I eat cereal and play video games for as long as I can; until I get a headache, until I feel like I'm going to black out from starvation, sometimes I have to pee for hours but just keep on playing. It's too hot to go out in the day, I don't have a car, and there's no school. In September, I will take four classes at Pasadena City College, and that's enough for now.

Almost everyday, Raff pounds on my locked bedroom door because he wants to play too. Sometimes I let him on Super Mario World two-player with me, or NHL Hockey, but I usually ignore him, and after a while he goes away.

I let my beard grow big, and when I check myself in the mirror, I look freaky.

"You'll never find employment with a beard like that," my mother says in Armenian, her good language.

"Good," I tell her.

Then, after dark Raider picks me up. This is when my day actually starts. We hang, drive around, waiting for Joker's work to end. Everyone calls Abo Joker now.

Joker isn't going to college. His grades weren't good, and he hates school anyway. He has a job on graveyard shift at Tommy Burgers Drive-Thru, serving late night burgers to stoners, people who can't sleep and kids like us. He says he likes it because he doesn't want to wake up early, but he looks worn down these days. Around three am we drag him out of Tommy Burgers. If he can stand at all, we get some free chili fries and drive up to the big wall at the Sepulveda Flood Basin or to this fucked up 24 hour arcade and porn shop. A lot of time, though, Joker has had enough. He bitches about how his feet hurt, and we all go home.

- The jacket

It's four weeks after I start at Pasadena City that Raff has his puffy Kings jacket stolen. Not one of those cheesy old purple and gold ones, this has the new Kings colors, silver and black. Joker and I bought him that jacket for a birthday gift. Poor kid was walking in the Glendale Galleria when four cholos, way older and bigger, walk up to him. "Give us your Kings jacket," they tell him, "or we will beat you right here, right now." Raff gives up his jacket.

That's the best story we can get anyway; Raff gets sketchy on the details. When my father finds out, he puts on his quiet, red face for dinner. Me, I keep talking. "We'll find those fucks and your jacket back," I keep saying. Finally, my father tells me to be quiet and eat. I'm already in trouble with him because I dropped one of my classes, so I shut up and stare at my plate.

Later I tell Joker the story, and we both decide to hate fucking cholos; it's that simple. I walk around staring at Mexican guys, daring them to get near me. Now I see enemies everywhere, so I finally join Armenian Power like Raider said I would. For my initiation I choose to fight fat Macaroni aka Mike. We stand there and hit each other for a minute, but it feels like an hour, and by the time the fight's over my chest aches and I feel weak.

"You were holding your breath the whole time, that's why you're dizzy," says Raider. "Now we should pick a tag for you." He's happy, I can tell, that his prophecy of me joining finally came true.

But no one can think of a tag until two weeks later when Joker tells that story of how I wrote my love poem to Emma Norsigian in junior high school. I am red in the face, and the boys can see that so they start to call me Romeo, but Joker says no. He says my tag should be Poet, which is better than Romeo anyway, and it sticks.

Raider promises us that we will get revenge on those motherfucker cholos someday. I start to late-night cruise with him again, like I used to do before college. I dress more in the AP style: baggy black jeans, gold rings, hockey shirts. I buy a Kings jacket so I can tempt fate. I skip classes and don't do homework. Why would I? Homework can't touch the low down belly feel I get when I think of my little brother scared at the hands of four big punks. Violation is the technical word for it. Our nights become a stand against violation. We pick up Joker from Tommy Burgers and cruise the streets in Raider's truck with that gun sitting there, almost out in the open. Oh yes, you could say we are looking for trouble, or maybe waiting for it to come to us. Three angry Hye Deghak.

-Weight training

I don't know if it's the long hours at the store or something else, but my father hardly talks. You could say he is enigmatic. I guess I started talking to make up for his quiet. So it's unlike father- unlike son. Raff was a talker too, until the jacket thing. But even my father has to say something when he sees my midterm grades. "If you don't want to stay in college, then you can get a job. Get a job and move out."

"I can't get a job. I'm in school."

He's like: "Two classes don't count as school."

My mother makes a noise like she's going to stop us but doesn't.

"Three classes," I tell him.

"One of your classes is gym training."

"Weight training."

"Weight training. This is not academic. It's not a true class. You are now a part time student. It even says on the papers they sent."

"Then I'll get a job," I snap back.

The louder I talk, the more quiet he becomes. "When will you get this job?"

"I don't know!" I yell at him, but inside I feel a little better. I get to take the weight of my anger and lay it on my father, or maybe we get to share it like a stone balanced on both our chests. Maybe that stresses him. So fuck, that's what I want. I want him to holler at me. I want him to say something instead of sitting there with his flat face. To him, I guess, it's a chess game. If he gets angry, he loses. Or maybe he doesn't care. I don't know.

Walk out- that's all I need to do. Just sit in a passenger seat of the black Ford Bronco, watch the night streets of LA pass by tinted windows as bass from high definition speakers crawls up and down the cab walls.

-That fucked Saturday night

It's 2:30 in the am and hot sky has returned. We are in the middle of a fierce December heat wave. Each day the sun rises like it's going to kick your ass, and dust is baked onto everything. Van Nuys winter.

Raider and I are on our way to pick up Joker. My knees are aching. This is what happened: I tried a new machine at weight training class. You lay down, put your feet against a lever and push until your legs can't go anymore. It's supposed to give you cut-up calves and thighs, but I should have been suspicious because it looked like a torture machine, and my legs feel like they were tortured. "Poet, you walk like a gimp man," is what Raider keeps telling me.

These days, picking up Joker is not a pretty sight. He's on grills shift and walks around smelling like beef. He has purple skin under his eyes and doesn't tell jokes like he used to.

Gabriel is the guy who works late night register at Tommy Burgers. He is not Mexican but Salvadoran; Joker told us that he fought in the jungle wars of El Salvador, which is a tiny country, smaller than California, smaller than Armenia.

Gabriel nods at us, "You want food?"

"No, we're here for the Joker."

He points behind a wall of cardboard boxes, pickle buckets and deep fryer gear. We've never gone back there, but we know there's a tiny bathroom where Joker is peeling off his cook pants and putting on sweats.

"Poet, you walk funny", Gabriel says to me. I want to give him shit for saying this, but we're all a little freaked out by the jungle warfare story.

Raider stares bullets at Gabriel as we wait for Joker who finally comes out from behind the counter, his hair all kinky and greased. "Free," he says, pulling up his shirt and scratching his belly. "Free at last! Free at last!" Doing his best MLK speech impersonation. He stops for a second to check me out, "Hey gimpo!"

"That Gabriel guy creeps me," says Raider, "let's go."

Now 3 am, I massage my knees as we cruise. Raider opens the windows all the way and cranks the AC. I turn the radio to Power 106, waiting for the Baker Boyz program to start. Joker's in the back seat; his face is crusty and white. Even with the air on, sweat slides down his neck and onto the leather seat. He should change his name from Joker to Sleepy I tell him.

He's like: "No. I'm still Joker."

"Yeah," says Raider, "a fucking joke."

"You're Sleepy," I say again.

Joker laughs. "I could have been one of the seven dwarves: Sleepy, Angry, Horny, Itchy, Bitchy and Bushy."

"That's six," I say.

We pull up to a red light and to our right is a rusted-out Cadillac with two homey-vatos slouched in the front seat. "Fuck, I've never seen cholos up so early in the morning," Raider says.

"Maybe they have night jobs, like Joker," I say.

"Beaners don't have jobs," Raider says which sounds like an ass-backward insult because Raider doesn't work, and I don't either.

"Let's fuck with them," says Joker. He leans forward so that his head is stuck between the front seats. "I think I've seen them before. They're local."

Raider looks back at Joker like he's about to ask a question but never gets the chance. Instead, Joker reaches down and pulls out the gun. He dives forward until he's almost laying on top of me, stretching the piece out the window. "Hey look at me!" he yells at the cholos.

It takes them a second to realize what's going on. It takes me a second to realize what's going on.

Suddenly the cholos are hollering at us in Spanglish. The driver is a short kid with a black mustache and he keeps saying, "Jesus! Jesus!" Which is funny because there is a Jesus tattoo on his shoulder. It's a tat of the 500 foot Jesus from Brazil, arms spread like a bird. The other cholo on the passenger side, I can't make out too well; he's bigger and has a black ball cap on.

Joker's arm is out the window, and his elbow is in my face. He curses back at the cholos in fucked up Armenian, "Eshoo Tzak!" He's pushing the buttons of everyone. If he misfires, then somebody's dead for sure.

The Jesus tattoo kid hits the gas.

I'm afraid, and I'm not ashamed to admit it. I'm afraid that Joker's going to shoot them, or that he's going to shoot me or that we'll get arrested. Hye Deghak don't go to jail.

Only Raider seems cool. He reaches over and yanks Joker by the shoulder and then goes for the gun. He does it fast, and for a second everyone has a hand on it. I have some of the barrel, Joker has the trigger, and Raider has a grip on the handle. "Don't drop it," I'm yelling. I have to pee. The gun is shiny with sweat and grease from Joker's palm. The chrome reflects the street lights. Gunlight.

The trigger is not pulled. I consider this to be impossible, and all three of us freeze for a moment holding our breaths and waiting for a blast and blood. Doesn't happen. Like a magic trick, Raider has his gun safely in hand.

Now the Caddy is far ahead of us, making good the cholos' escape. They run one red light and then another when they get hit by a white Toyota crossing the other way. Both cars go skidding with a metal scream.

"Oh fuck- you see that?" says Joker, going on like it was something on TV. As if we could miss it.

Raider stares for a moment, his face blank in the same way it was when he was watching Gabriel the Salvadoran. He busts a u-turn. I swivel in my seat so I can look out the back window, and I see the Jesus tattoo kid getting out of the Caddy. He looks fucked up, walking real slow and bent over. The ball cap guy is still in the car, waving his hands around like he's swatting flies. Raider cuts left to get us onto the 101, and I lose sight of it all.

Raider starts to curse. "Fucking ass! Dumb motherfucker!" He puts the gun back in its place.

For me, I laugh. This is surprising. Maybe I'm just too tired to deal. Maybe I'm onto Joker's wavelength. I don't know but I'm laughing: Hohoho! Like Santa.

So Raider drives us home, all the time talking to himself because no one is allowed to touch the gun without his permission.

Even though I'm laughing, I feel a cold illness sitting between my balls and belly. When I get home, I throw up and do my best to forget.

-After the gun

My aching knees slowly heal and Joker, aka Abo Tavidagian, gets his ass kicked like you think it would happen, down late one night in the parking lot. He goes out to sweep Tommy Burger napkins and spilled fries, and someone hits him with something, a pool stick maybe, or a cane. Joker barely has time to turn around before he's jumped.

He sees three or four cholos, maybe the ones from the Caddy incident, but maybe not. He can't make out details too well. He remembers some guy with a bandanna, another with gold teeth, a fat guy with no shirt and gothic tats all over his big old titties. To give Joker credit, he goes down swinging; he lays a roundhouse into one of those chumps. But in the end, they put him away nice.

Joker's parents call and Raff gets the story. He knocks on the door of my room, and I tell him to go away because I think he wants to play video games.

"Joker just got beat up. He's at the hospital," Raff says through the door.

Now I feel like shit. I rush to let him in, but by the time I get there he's cleared out. "Sorry!" I yell down the hall at his closed door.

I should be there to put my arm around my brother's shoulder. Instead I stand in an empty hall with fucked up orange-brown carpet. With my parents at the store and the nintendo on pause, our house seems dead. I can hear cars moving down the street, and a clock ticking in the living room. I get a flash of that ill feeling again, the same one I had on the night of the gun, and it reminds me of how bad it can be when you are fearful. I suddenly want my ADD pills. At any moment the walls could close in. The lights could go black. These are things you never want to be reminded of.

-Now again

Before the job interview at the gym, I swing by Joker's place with the new Sports Illustrated. His mother lets me in. She wears one of those flower dresses that all mothers have. He's been back from the hospital two weeks now. He's slouched up in bed, watching TV, and he looks well rested-like some sickness has come out of his system. Well rested and abused at the same time with cuts, stitches and bruises. Looking once again like the comic book Joker who's just lost a fight with Batman.

"You're wearing a shirt and tie. You're here to lecture me? I already got a lecture from Raider," he says. "Next time, I'm going to get my own gun. Kill those perturbed motherfucker beaners."

"Do you even know what perturbed means?"

"Fuck you."

I'm like: "I just came over to read you Sports Illustrated. The new one."

He rips the magazine out of my hands. "I'm not an invalid. I got my ass kicked, but I can still read." Opens to a hockey article and there's a photo of notorious roughneck Marty McSorely giving someone a brutal check. Blood on the glassboard, that kind of check. "That's me," says Joker, pointing to the bloody player who is some unknown guy on the New York Islanders. "How come you bring me Sport Illustrated? I mean, why not Playboy? You're a poet, why don't you bring me poems?"

"You hate poems."

"Nah. There was one I liked." Joker leans back in bed so his head is almost buried in pillows. "There was this poem about an Indian shooting an arrow at the moon. From sixth grade, do you remember?"

"At the moon?"

"*The arrow and the moon out there, in the pale cold air.* From sixth grade." He puts up one finger like he's pointing to where the moon could be.

"Why would I remember that?"

"You're the poet."

"Hey, you're not really going to get a gun? You're too crazy to get one."

"Why are you wearing a tie?" he says.

"I'm going to get a job."

"Your parents made you?"

"No."

"You scared?" he laughs at me. "Fuck you. I'm not going to get a gun and you're not going to get a job with a tie. That's reciprocity. And I know what that word means."

"No Joker, it's not like that. I need cash. Cash-money. And it's at a gym so I can work out for free," I hope he'll believe a half-ass lie, but what else can I say- *No, I'm afraid of ending up like you, working a dead end job at Tommy Burgers, picking fights and getting beat?* "I need the money," I say again.

"Go make lots of money then, maybe I'll rob you." He makes a gun with his finger and thumb. Aims at me. "Bang! You're dead." Then he puts it to his own skull. "Bango! Just blew my head off."

I can't say anything.

He sees me frozen and says, "Okay Armen, go get the job."

"Thanks," I tell him. "Thanks."

"And I get a gun," he says.

I try to laugh the whole thing off, but I feel like there's an invisible chain pulling me out of his bedroom. I stumble around his bed to the door, and I can't say goodbye fast enough now.

-Long long ago

There is a boy in a school yard at recess. His name is Abo Tavidagian. We are at the Hayestan Church Summer Camp which is free to all children of Armenian descent. There is no yard so the playground is also the parking lot. The boy says, "Pretend to be a dog!"

"No way."

So he gets on his hands and knees and barks and bites me.

I run for the teacher. I've never seen anything as crazy as this.

He laughs at me.

I stop running, pretend to be a dog and bite him back. We will become friends I think.

Bringing Ararat

Bringing Ararat first appeared in The Missouri Review.

On the Friday that they received the money from his father, Harrut had gone for a swim. He got off work in the early afternoon, stripped to his boxer shorts and dove, crashing through some shallow waves, into the sea. He was athletic, with a long, lean body and could kick out great distances. The water off Beirut was warm for most of the year, and he would sometimes bring a net and knife in case he was lucky and found a patch of sea urchins that he could pick and sell to a young Syrian street vendor. Or sometimes he would cut the urchins' mottled shells and suck down the raw, salty flesh; the texture it left in his mouth was somewhere between steak and cream.

This time he didn't look for urchins. Instead he closed his eyes and felt the warm water rushing over his chest and groin. He went out several hundred yards, until his calves burned and sea foam hissed, dissolving in his ears, and then he turned to face the city, with its endless mix of shanty and establishment. This was 1964, before the militias and economic snafus, when people called Beirut the "Paris of the East." Somewhere behind the waterfront and the birds and vendors was the apartment he shared with his sister, knots of highway passes being built, and beyond that, Sirin's, his girlfriend's, apartment with its wide front porch. Banks, restaurants, churches, and people everywhere, coming and going.

When he came home, he found Flori, his sister, cooking: grilled lamb with salt and pepper; its fatty aroma hung in the air. She wasn't much for housework, but she liked cooking. On the counter beside her there was a large, opened envelope, and she was smiling. News, Harrut thought. Flori always smiled when there was news of some kind—good or bad- it didn't matter. It was an attribute she shared with many of the women in their extended clan, the group of people that Harrut simply thought of as the Family—the way things were dealt with before modern psychology came to the fore: the women generally smiled, and the men were generally reserved.

He walked into Flori's maybe-good-maybe-bad smile with a sense of tension. He gave her the usual kiss, crossing from one cheek to the other. "God, you should have seen the birds down at the shore today. Millions. They were fighting and screaming," he said. They usually spoke in Armenian but could switch to Romanian, not common in the area, if they wanted privacy.

He walked past her to the icebox and fished out a jug of pickled vegetables. He forked into the mass, picking out carrots and cauliflower. He made a lot of noise eating.

Flori laughed at the way he ate, laughed at how he loved his meals. She was seventeen, seven years his junior, but her personality vacillated; at times she seemed twelve, at others, thirty. Sometimes Harrut could not believe that this dyed blonde who wore American-movie-inspired dresses with silver clasps was his sister. On the increasingly rare occasions when he went to restaurants with both Flori and Sirin, he would imagine that he had somehow fallen into a Hollywood film with a lovely starlet on either side. He would notice other men watching jealously.

"Do you want?" He thrust a forkful of cauliflower at her.

She handed the envelope to him. It was covered with stamps in English, Arabic and French. The letter wasn't much of a letter, really—only a few paragraphs in his father's hand.

Dear Son,

Your mother is worried about you. She thinks your girlfriend cannot be the right woman for you. I have tried to tell her how it is with men and that it is nothing, but you know how she never listens. I think that you know that this relationship with this Lebanese woman should end, and that we expect you in New York soon. Use the enclosed money. Keep Flori well and write back.

In her big, looping handwriting, his mother had added: *Everyone is well. Manole is well. Anahit was sick again, a little, but she is feeling better. Ardash and his family are well, but his son, Calust, has become an angry hothead. There are so many poor people here, more than Bucharest. I will send you candy.*

There were photographs: about half a dozen color shots on heavy paper, and then there was the money. It wasn't in the envelope; Flori had it in her other hand. She warily held it out to him, a wad of green wrapped in mint-scented wax paper. "We can go now," she said.

He pulled the cash out of her fist, unwrapped the wax paper and rifled through it. There was over a thousand dollars, American—easily enough for two flights to New York.

"Half for you and half for me," she said.

His father had wrapped it in the mint paper, he was sure, because of his distrust of government agencies. It reminded him of how he had watched his father hide gold in their suitcases about a year before. "Well, we'll see," Harrut said and stuffed it into his pocket.

She glared at him. "It's not yours!"

"I know, I'll hold onto it until we're ready to go."

"I am ready to go. I'm going to buy a ticket tomorrow."

Harrut shook his head. "Are you crazy? You can't go alone." Women simply did not travel alone. Why was this? Out of safety. Out of respect for tradition. It was another in a millennium-long string of traditions. There was a sense of shame that went with a woman who traveled by herself. Of course they both also understood that there was a sense of shame that came when your father called for you and you didn't come.

Flori said, "We'll go together. Don't you want to be happy?"

"I don't know. You can't go by yourself."

"Harrut, are you crazy? Is that girl making you promise to stay?"

He shook his head.

"How can you do this, after everything you've been given?"

"I work hard for everything I have. Everything we have." He indicated the kitchen, their apartment, their sturdy furniture. But he had vague notions that she meant something else, some debt he owed his family, the Family. The feeling made him edgy. He didn't mind owing money or even favors—things that could be paid back in clean ways— but he didn't like the idea of people shuffling his life based on debts that couldn't be paid.

"Then what is it?" she said.

"Here. I want to stay here."

"Here? In this kitchen?" She did an angry laugh.

He watched her go back to the lamb. She drew her shoulders in tight, and her breath came out in a sharp way. They had been through this before, but never with the money staring them in the face. He pretended not to notice Flori's remark and turned his attention to the photos. He lifted and held them in a sort of fan, as though playing cards. There was Manole, his father's brother and business partner, in something of a cinema vérité shot, with his white barber's jacket, scissors poised over someone's half-bald head. There was Ardash too, his father's mustachioed cousin, yet another barber, on a crowded beach. Coney Island?

Another picture of their parents, standing side by side, unsmiling—quite different from one another and yet each royal in their own way. Onig was thin, a flashy dresser who wore sport coats and sometimes, a captain's hat. He had the presence of a man who was just going to or coming back from the yacht club, not a barber shop. He chose his reading glasses with great care and looked something of a dandy.

Bytsar was their mother, and she was queenly—a large woman with a large bosom who kept her hair short and dyed, usually red. She liked bright colors and often wore Turkish-style slippers at home and eccentric hats when she went out. She was not polite and could send up huge volleys of curses in Armenian. She was the only woman in their family who cursed openly. She'd been hijacked, she sometimes told them, by history and family and her husband, and the world could eat her shit.

They did look royal, but Harrut was beginning to notice something new in these occasional letters and photographs from New York. He was feeling the steely persistence of two people who had endured a genocide and two world wars.

He knew Bytsar had watched two Turkish soldiers rip her father's feet open with the claw sides of their hammers; then they had to walk out of their town. Her father had never said a word she claimed. He just whispered to himself, walking and waiting to die.

Onig had spent the last half of World War II crouched in a machine-gun nest with his brother, Manole. During the brief postwar anarchy they'd sold their guns and ammunition to the black market. Onig never spoke about it; only through Manole did Harrut finally hear the story.

They ate salt-and-pepper lamb in silence, and after Flori had retreated to her room and turned on her radio, Harrut put the photos and letters back into the envelope and then hunted through the kitchen until he found a half-empty tea tin. He buried the money under the tea leaves and hid the tin under his bed, hoping that Flori wouldn't think to look there, but suspecting that she could easily find it if she wanted. He wished the money had never come. He squatted down and peered underneath to make sure the tin was far out of sight, but he felt its presence, like a bomb.

There was an unwritten law that his family had to move. It had begun in Turkey, when the soldiers came, and it wouldn't stop until . . . well, that was Harrut's question. All of them, an entire ghetto, a clan plucked from the countryside and transported, somehow becoming middle class in transit: big noses, fat guts, strong shoulders, kinky hair, suitcases with smuggled gold, brown eyes, eyebrows in the shape of curling smoke, bejeweled Middle Eastern-style slippers, iron-gripped handshakes, perpetually in transit. If only they could have brought Ararat with them, the white-head mountain of Noah; it might have anchored his people.

Monday. Going back to work after the money came brought relief for Harrut. He liked to be there, cramming numbers on his notepad or ordering the marker man just a few feet to one side or the other. He took off his tie and construction hat, barely aware of angry motorists on either side, and let the sunlight wash him. He leaned forward and fixed his viewfinder, found his mark and allowed himself to get lost in the city scenes that presented themselves. Grey stucco buildings, market stalls that had occupied the same corner for centuries, a rare pack camel, veiled women, women in bright, short skirts.

He didn't want to go directly home and decided, instead, to spend the evening with Sirin. He called Flori and told her he was going on a date. If she needed it, there was some money in the tiny phone stand in their living room. He paused, suddenly guilty from bringing up the idea of hidden money.

"I'll be fine," Flori snapped before hanging up on him.

Sirin was waiting on her front doorstep. "I thought maybe you weren't coming," she said. She was Lebanese but had grown up in an Armenian neighborhood and spoke the language well, although with a distinct rolling accent. She also spoke French, and a local dialect of Arabic. Harrut spoke Romanian, Armenian and some Russian. Armenian was the one language they shared.

"Of course I was coming." He took her hand. They were in love. Not in the modern version of love; they had little empathy, but they didn't expect empathy, and they weren't having sex, which they understood as something for after marriage. Both had grown up in households where parents performed clearly outlined roles. They understood that as a young couple, the best chance for happiness came from the coming together of a handsome man and pretty woman who shared a common class: similar education, breeding, and background. They did not need their love confirmed outside of their roles as a man and woman. It was all confirmed by friends and relatives who saw them walking together and said, "There goes a happy couple." She would keep the house, and he would earn money. It was understood.

At the restaurant, Sirin told Harrut about how she had taken Parrig, her little pug-nosed dog, out for a walk and how he had once again slipped his collar and nearly run away.

"The dog," he said. He told her to get a tighter collar but suspected that she never would. More than a few times he had been there when Parrig had done his escape act, panting and bug-eyed, on a crowded street. Sirin would always run after, smiling, and Harrut was obliged to chase them both, yelling for her to watch out for a car or bicycle. Miraculously no one had been hurt on these occasions. In fact, Sirin would usually be in good spirits for the rest of the day.

"A tighter collar," she said in agreeable voice. "But I'm afraid he will choke."

"He will learn to obey," Harrut said.

"Did you swim today, Harrut?"

"A few day ago."

She tapped her strong nails on the table a few times. "They are still asking you to come to New York?"

"They are. Flori wants to go."

"Then are you going to leave me?" She made it into a half joke, pouting as she spoke.

"No." At that moment, he made the decision to not tell her about the money.

She put her hand over his. "What's Flori going to do? Where is she tonight?"

"She was tired. She wanted to stay home."

Sirin let the subject go, and they quietly picked at the warm flatbread in front of them. Harrut let himself look at her, the femininity he saw in her frame. He carried a set of images of Sirin, a mental photo-mosaic: her rounded face, curly brown hair, strong thighs. These images could bring back the same feeling of amour he'd had when they first met at a dance hall that was strung with gold and violet lights. From that feeling, it was easy to see why he shouldn't leave Beirut.

"Where did you swim?" she finally asked.

"By the warehouses, at dusk. It was nice to be away from people."

"That's why I like you so much, Harrut. You are a tough guy," she laughed. "I remember when we went to the beach and you went so far out that I thought you had drowned." She had called the police, and he had come back to shore to find two put-upon looking officers.

The waiter came with a pitcher of ice water, a plate of cheese and a new plate of bread cut thin but very wide. The ends of the bread hung off the sides of the plate. After he left, Harrut leaned very close to Sirin, using his shoulder to create a triangle of privacy, and kissed her. She opened herself to the kiss in a very passive way, the proper response for the time and place.

After, he walked her home. He saw her parents stationed on the wide front porch, where they could watch their return. Harrut waved to them, and they waved back. He imagined how his own parents might watch Sirin, unsmiling, and not wave back to her.

By the time he got home Flori was asleep, and Harrut was grateful because he didn't want to talk. He wondered if she'd gone into his room and found the money. If she had counted it to make sure it was all there. He slipped into the kitchen for a glass of seltzer.

From his vantage point, Harrut could see the telephone in the living room, black and bony and threatening to ring. How many time zones was it to New York? It was early morning there, he reckoned; cars would have begun to rumble in the streets outside his parents' apartment.

Then, in a moment that Harrut later dismissed as late-night foolishness, he opened the cutlery drawer and fished out a cloth napkin, one with blue embroidered grape clusters. He took it and carefully draped it over the telephone. "Out of sight," he said to the phone, "out of mind." Then he went to bed.

After the genocide, his family had settled in a small town on the Romanian side of the Black Sea, where Harrut was born. And again, with the coming of the Russians, they went to Bucharest. They lasted fourteen years in Bucharest; it was where he'd grown up, so it had seemed permanent, but that was an illusion. A wonderful illusion, though. In Bucharest, Harrut reached amazing heights of stability and productivity that appealed to the linear aspect of his personality and made him proud. He was a good student, studying metallurgy at the Polytechnic, an ace football player (soccer, not American); he worked as a movie projectionist in the evenings and could take his friends to the movies for free.

Harrut was also, although only subconsciously aware of it, comforted by all the things that the women in his family gave: hot meals, a font of gossip and neighborhood news, a sense that their home was filled with life.

His family, the Family, filled in a tight-knit ethnic ghetto on the north side of the city. It was not unusual for Harrut to find himself at a holiday party with some hundred people, half of whom he was somehow related to.

At these gatherings, the oldest, some of whom still spoke Turkish, had their table and the teens had theirs, where the boys could yell at each other and the girls could mock the boys. There was a table for parents and one for small children, who tried to find any excuse to get to the teenage table. People would come and go, maybe borrowing a car to take little Araxi home early, or someone would head down the street to drop off leftovers for Ilona's dogs and goats.

Harrut and some of the other boys, usually Vahe and Hagop, would run into the kitchen, which bustled with ten or fifteen cooking matriarchs and was filled with the scent of scallions, feta, baked beef, pickled cabbage. "Zho," Harrut's mother warned them. "Devils, get out!" But the other women would take pity, and the boys would walk out clutching plates stacked high with appetizers and anything else that was prepared early. They would holler at the girls, showing off their swag.

"You're going to eat that?" the girls would say. "You're going to get fat!"

And the boys, in response, would already be eating and holding their stomachs, exaggerating their bloatedness. They always ate before anything was officially served, which allowed them to run off early. If the day was nice, they rode in Hagop's car.

"Man," Hagop would say, stroking his scraggly beard. He said "man" in English, imitating the British pop stars. "Man," then switching to Armenian, "I tell you there is only one girl for me."

"Brigitte Bardot!" the boys inevitably hollered over the engine. They always wound up turning out of the city onto a busted-up country road.

"Harrut, do you have a picture of her from the theater?"

Sometimes, Harrut would take a poster or two from work. He could sell them to his friends for a few dollars. His friends liked the comedians and the action heroes, of course, but they really liked the women, especially the French ones.

"You cannot steal a Bardot poster," he said. "It's like stealing the Mona Lisa."

"Brigitte Bardot!" yelled another one of the boys.

They talked about football, which Harrut played at school alongside the sons of Communist leaders. The other boys admired him for this, just as they admired Hagop for his car and British-style clothes.

Nights in his room, Harrut would sleep dreamlessly or dream about playing football, scoring a goal, running, bursts of color.

The day that Onig said they were leaving Bucharest, Harrut came home to an acrid smell. The dining room table was defaced, scarred and blistered, and he realized that it had been set on fire. Flori was smiling, making coffee as though nothing had happened, and Harrut knew the fire must have been his mother's doing. If it had been anyone else, if it had been an accident, Flori would have rushed to tell him the story.

He passed his father, who was settled over a newspaper in the family room. He began to climb the stairs to his bedroom, but Onig called him back.

Onig asked several questions about the Polytechnic and the football team. Harrut answered directly. The tone of their conversations had been set when Harrut was six and Onig would not address his son as anything but an adult. Their conversations had always been straightforward affairs with little space for asides or levity; things were simply this way or that- like two businessmen speaking.

Finally, Onig leaned forward, adjusting his navy blazer and said, "We are moving to New York. I am bribing some people."

Harrut smiled without showing his teeth.

His father explained further: The government had raised taxes. Agents had come, threatening to turn the barber shop into a "public enterprise." Onig's plan was to get exit visas to Beirut, which was not difficult; and from Lebanon, as he understood it, it was mere formality to gain visas to New York, where refugees from the Eastern Bloc were quite welcome.

After, Harrut realized that he should have seen it coming. Already a few of their more distant kin had left for Beirut and then France or the United States. They sent encouraging letters to his parents. He should have seen it coming.

Onig stared at him through his thin, spotless glasses. Harrut noticed, for the first time, that his father had almost no eyebrows, just a fine shadow of hair there. He was surprised by this because he and his mother and Flori all had thick, dark eyebrows. He was also surprised that he had never noticed this. Was it a recent development?

"Your mother is not so happy to move. You talk to her and tell her how much you would like to go," Onig said.

But the truth was soon revealed, over a dinner of dolmha warmed in broth, that Bytsar didn't mind going. At least, she didn't mind it enough to set the dinner table ablaze. What had set her off was the fact that she had not been consulted.

"When did you decide this?" she demanded of her husband as she poured another ladleful of broth over his meal. "Did you decide this in a dream?"

He glared back icily. "Madam," he said. He called her "Madam" when they fought. "Madam, I had no choice."

Harrut saw it as his duty to tell his mother the reasons that they should move to New York, but he simply couldn't think of anything to say, and he was relieved when Flori, who was enthralled with the idea, jumped in to describe it as a city of fine dining and ubiquitous wealth. It was, in fact, Flori, and not the men of the family, who ultimately consoled Bytsar's hurt sense of self and sold her on New York.

Harrut didn't eat much. He made a mental list of the things he loved about Bucharest: college, football, the musty projection booth at the movie theater and more than all that, the establishment of himself: the sense that his life was woven intrinsically into the cityscape around him. He pictured the college clubhouse, his small bedroom on the second floor, the movie theater, empty after the last film had closed, all catching fire one by one, shriveling like photos left in a hearth.

His father ate, stirring his stew, adding pepper, stirring again and then quietly taking a spoonful.

By late August their exit visas were approved, and then government agents came and made Onig sign over the rights to his house and barber shop.

Onig bought as much gold and jewelry as he could and had Harrut help him stash it in the bottoms of their suitcases. Over these they folded their clothes in thick layers. Harrut watched his father work in a quick, steady way. Onig never removed his tie. He never broke a sweat. Harrut thought his father looked a little like some international spy in a movie, but it was more owing to apathy on the part of airport security that the scheme worked. They had made it onto the plane without ever having their baggage checked. Harrut had never been on a plane before, and as it took off he clenched his armrests and took a deep breath, like he was going underwater.

Beirut did not welcome them. They arrived in the midst of a recession that fueled resentment against outsiders, and work was nearly impossible to find. The early fall was punctuated by a blistering heat wave. The exit process to New York was more complicated than Onig had figured; the Americans, it turned out, required as much red tape as the Communists. It would take over a year to get the okay to emigrate.

In the mean time, they settled into a shabby one-bedroom apartment that became a way station for other Romanian-Armenian immigrants. Friends and family would stay over until they could find their own place. Without work, Harrut felt a dragging sense of shame, and he kept to himself. He would wander the city for hours, dreading the thought of coming home. Sometimes he would wake up early in the mornings and stumble, high-stepping over relatives snoring on the floor, to the bathroom, where he would convince himself to shave. He wasn't particularly creative in the way of metaphors, but he imagined that his straight razor was a sword cutting away at the murk of sleep. He liked the abrasive sting of shaving, in the same way he liked diving into cold water.

A few months before they were scheduled to leave, Harrut found a job funded by a lucrative public development contract, a government plan to replace the city's crooked lanes with bright highways. Because of the work, his parents had gone to New York without him, the plan being that he would follow after the contract had ended. Flori was left behind with him because in some ways she was still regarded as a child, and it would be easier to send for her after they had settled in. But the government extended the contract; it seemed the project was never-ending, and then Harrut was promoted to road surveyor, and then he met Sirin at a dance hall and there was yet another contract extension, during which Harrut was enrolled into the union, and another year had passed.

In the morning, Flori held up the grape-embroidered cloth napkin. "Did you get drunk last night, Harrut? You put the phone to bed."

"It was a joke," he said.

"A joke? Did you go drink with Sirin?"

"No. She's a good girl, and I wish you would be nice about her. She always asks about you."

"You're going to see her again?"

On their next date Sirin said to Harrut, "You won't discuss your parents with me. That means something must be wrong."

"I have this pain in my back," he suddenly said. He was surprised that he said this. It was another impulsive thing, like putting the phone to bed. It seemed he was becoming more likely to do or say random, unrehearsed things. It was also a lie; his back didn't hurt, but it was the closest he'd ever come to admitting he was torn about things, that the same rules that kept Flori from stealing the money under his bed and going to New York on her own were also refusing to let him disobey his father.

"You should have your back massaged. I'll massage you," she said.

"Where?" he said, meaning surely she wasn't going to give him a massage right there in the restaurant.

But she did. She reached right across the small table, oblivious to the crowd of diners, and grabbed the corners of his starched shirt. She massaged his shoulders, which was out of character for both of them—for her to do it in public and for Harrut to accept. He focused on her hands. He did not look at her face. He cocked his head at an angle to see her fingers, which were clean, strong, with white, moon-shaped lunulae.

"Did you have a hard day?" she said.

He shook his head.

"I feel bad, Harrut. I feel bad because I'm keeping your sister from her family."

"No," he said. "It's not you."

"Why don't you let her go? If you're happy to stay, you stay. If she's happy to go, she goes. I know she can't go by herself, but you could take her and then come back."

"It's not so simple."

"Yes it is." For the first time ever, he saw that she was angry with him. "Flori's unhappy. It makes you unhappy. In New York, at least she can find friends or maybe a boyfriend to be with." After a few moments she added, "Are you happy to stay?"

He said yes, as he had before, and said he would stay.

Her fingers held onto his shoulders in a way that to Harrut seemed too erotic for a restaurant. "My parents love you. I love you."

"I love you," he said.

"If you loved your sister, you would take her to New York. I have a picture of you in my head. Harrut, you could be a hero."

"What hero?" he teased her. "Don Quixote?"

"Don Quixote would make the right decision."

"The same Don Quixote who declared that a flock of sheep was the pagan army of Alifanfaron?"

One night an electric impulse wended its way through the roughly seven thousand miles of phone line that separated New York from Beirut, and the phone did ring; it was their mother. She asked how they were and if they'd received the candies and gum she'd sent. Then she complained about New York and its effects on their men kinfolk. "They say they're going to buy an apartment building!" She was nearly yelling, as though she had to talk loud so that Harrut could hear her all those miles away. "It's an ugly gray building. Your father wants to talk to you."

"My son," Onig began; over the transatlantic cable, his voice sounded thin, in counterpoint to Bytsar's hollering. "Why are you not coming?"

Harrut blushed, and because men simply did not blush, he ordered Flori out of the room, and she fired a bitter smile at him as she left.

"You cannot be happy. Your mother is worried about that Lebanese woman."

"Tata!"

"Is she pregnant?"

"Of course not!"

"Well, good. Then come to New York. I know you don't like to move. I know how you are stubborn and quiet, but I know that you are that way because you are like me. I promise you that New York is the last place we go. Use the money I sent. This is the best place, and you can have a car. You can afford your own home, in New Jersey."

Harrut began to see some fuzzy images of a possible life in New York. "I'll think," he said.

"You still have the money?"

"Yes!"

"What are you going to do? Everyone is here. You have to come."

Harrut clenched the phone, trying hard to find the power to say no to his father. The power did not come, and he simply repeated that he would think.

"You hurt your family, son." Onig said it without any admonition, as though he was reporting the evening news. Then he hung up, and Harrut could hear the faint exit hiss of those thousands of miles of phone line. It was like a hissing snake quickly moving away. When it faded to a dial tone, he realized that Flori was watching him. She'd come back while his back was turned.

"Abush!" she said—Armenian for "Moron!" Her eyes flickered under her thick bangs.

"I'm going swimming."

"Swimming, swimming! Can't you do anything else? What are you, a duck?" She crossed her arms and suddenly said, "I'm going with you."

She had never followed him before, and Harrut saw it as a sudden, strange gesture of compromise. He made an effort to talk to her on the way to the docks, not about New York but about his love for Beirut. He showed her the dance hall, decorated in strings of gold and violet lights, where he'd met Sirin. In the way of a good-natured joke, a doorman saluted them like a soldier. There was a Rolls-Royce parked in front, and the night air was warm with the smell of tobacco, and ocean salt.

That night Harrut swam out far, sometimes turning to look back at Flori's shadowy figure waiting for him on shore. When he came back, he lunged left then right, stretching his calves and thighs and said, "Every time we move I find some way to be happy, and then Tata says we have to go."

"Harrut, it's for the best," she said in the convincing way that teenagers simply sum things up. "If I go to New York, you would miss me?" she asked.

"Yes."

After he admitted that, she seemed content, and she stopped making him feel guilty about New York. She started a habit of coming with him to the docks at night. "Be careful," she would tell him.

But Harrut laughed and kept pushing out farther into the bay, until the one time he really did go out too far. That night the air was cool; he hardly noticed his body. He dug his forearms into the water, kicking and sometimes pulling his head over the surface to breathe. It was black out, and he kept the light of the city to his back. He stopped, treaded water for a moment and then turned back.

At that point he was simply tired, and it took him a precious minute to realize that he was swimming against a rip tide. He changed direction so that he could push perpendicular to the current—he knew of small loading pier, about a hundred yards to the north, where he could climb out of the sea. But his legs were beginning to feel rubbery, and when he made out the silhouette of a small sailboat nearby, he headed for it instead. Only when he was a few feet from the boat did he panic. He didn't expect to panic at all, and it came over him like a tremor. He was suddenly sure he was going to drown, and he splashed and hollered like a wet animal.

The boat floated the last few feet to him. A small, old-style lantern hung off the yardarm, and he saw a pair of hands, fat arms reaching over for him. Harrut's immediate reaction was that the boat was too small for his rescuer. The man was large and toadlike, with a wooden leg. He looked like a comedian pretending to be a pirate, and if Harrut had met him under some other circumstance, he would have certainly had to suppress a laugh. In this case, however, Harrut fought to catch his breath.

"You were out pretty far," the man said in French.

Harrut shook his head. His French was poor, and he spoke haltingly. "It was a terrible miscalculation," he tried to say.

The man roared at some grammatical error. "A miscalculation? Where did you come from?"

Harrut pointed a little to the south.

"Are you Armenian?"

Harrut nodded and coughed.

The big man chuckled again. Harrut noticed he was sitting at an awkward angle, so that he could use his wooden leg to casually fix the boat's rudder handle. "I thought you looked familiar." The man switched to Armenian. "My name is Sevag Nostonian. I think I've seen you before."

"You probably saw me if you have a car. I work for road construction."

"So you're the one who causes all the traffic."

"It's the city, they don't know how to plan things," Harrut said, gripping himself and trying not to break into a spasm of shivering. He prided himself on hardiness and was embarrassed by the idea of shivering.

"That's life. That's why I have this boat." Sevag gestured to the empty sea. He subtly twitched his leg and changed the direction of the sail.

Harrut spat overboard a few times. "The traffic is miserable."

"I wish I had a towel for you. But we will be back to land shortly."

Harrut couldn't think of anything else to say, so he thanked the man again and waited.

Finally, Sevag said, "I can't help but wonder where you're from. You have a little accent. Hungarian?"

"Romanian. I grew up in Bucharest. We left because of the idiot Communists. They ruined our business."

Sevag nodded sympathetically. "I've heard of you Romanian-Armenians. You're all headed for America, passed through here like a wave."

"Yes, that's where I'm supposed to go."

"But you don't want to?"

Harrut leaned forward, trying to get a better view of Sevag's face. It made him uncomfortable that this person had suddenly guessed his business.

Sevag's jaw was prevalent, thrust forward. "That must be the problem," he said. "Don't be surprised. I hear so many parents complain to me that their children don't want to leave."

"What matters is logical choice," Harrut said.

"What is the logical choice then? Do you go or stay?"

"Oh, you don't understand." Harrut threw his hands in the air.

"You don't want to go. That's why you swam so far. To drown yourself."

"Ridiculous."

"Hardly ridiculous. Why did you swim so far? You were shaking when I found you."

"You didn't find me, I found you," Harrut reminded him. He began to see that Sevag had some agenda, that he was going to make this into something larger than it was. He might have been a priest or a teacher. How else could he have heard all those parents complain about their children? But Harrut was pinned; obviously it would be insolent to ignore Sevag.

"It doesn't matter," Sevag said. "My point is that something must be troubling you. Nothing happens by mistake."

"My father is in New York, and he's called for me and my sister. I'm not sure it's the best decision. I have good work here. I have a girlfriend."

"There's a lot of money in New York, and women," Sevag said.

"But it's so far away, and I don't speak the language."

Sevag nodded. "Your family only means the best for you, I'm sure. What they do, they do for love." For some reason he pointed to his wooden leg.

Harrut shook his head.

"No, listen. Are your parents originally from Armenia?"

"It's Turkey now."

"My roots are from there too, almost at the Russian border. When the genocide came, the Turks shackled all the men by their ankles. I was just a boy then, a coward. I started to cry, but my father made me be quiet."

Harrut had heard of the shackles, of course, and the forced marches in the desert. Everyone had heard, but he was taken aback by the confession. It was one thing to tell your family—as Harrut had been told about the death of his maternal grandfather—but another to tell a total stranger. In the Romanian-Armenian community, or at least in his part of that community, revealing personal tragedy was the same as revealing personal weakness. Genocide stories were almost always kept secret. Sevag told how the Turkish soldiers didn't seem so bad at first. One had offered his father a cigarette. Sevag's family were told they were under house arrest and that later they would be moved to another village.

But in the morning the they took one of Sevag's uncles, and the men realized that they were going to be killed. The Turks had left them unguarded because they were shackled, but because Sevag was young, his ankle iron was loose.

Sevag's face was marked with lines that seemed to get deeper when he spoke. But he was smiling, too, a fat smile that suggested he found relief in his story, in the same way a priest might find relief in the story of crucifixion. He'd probably told this story a number of times, Harrut thought.

"My father came to me and grabbed me by the hair. He leaned over and pulled out a small knife he kept in his boot. For sure, I thought, I was dead. But he used the knife on my shackles. He tried to force them off. The other men joined in, and they nearly broke my foot. 'You'll have to cut there,' one of my uncles said.

"At first I didn't understand, but then I realized they meant to cut my foot, the fleshy part of my heel, so it could come free.

"Of course I started to yell and scream, and I guess we were lucky the Turks didn't come to see what the problem was. While the other men held me, my father cut off the back end of my heel, like how you cut the big end off a carrot. What a sight. I don't wish that for anyone."

He was careful to describe how his foot was wrapped in strips of cloth and how he'd put on his father's boots, which flopped loosely as he ran to his grandfather's farm.

Maybe Sevag was a liar, someone who told stories to make a point, but even if he was, the lie was not so far-fetched. Harrut knew what had happened to his own grandfather. For a moment he was mesmerized by the image of a fat, sobbing boy running down a road while his boot quickly filled with blood.

"The truth is that it was survival. If a family hurts itself, it's to survive. My father did it because he loved me, so I could carry on the name."

The two men spent the last few minutes of the trip in silence, Sevag's wooden leg occasionally clicking against the ship. When they landed, Sevag offered Harrut a cigarette, which he took even though he didn't smoke. He felt the urge to bow to the big man and was surprised when Sevag finally stood and revealed himself to be quite short. Harrut watched him for another moment and then walked off to where Flori and his towel were waiting. Partly because of his own physical reaction to nearly having drowned, but certainly also because of Sevag's story, he felt drunk.

He didn't tell his sister about Sevag; he didn't want to start a new argument about the money and New York. He only told her that he'd had to swim back to a different point because of the currents.

A heat wave was expected. There were announcements on the radio and in the newspaper. Harrut's work site would be closed for a week. These were the times when the city was forcefully reminded that it was only ten miles from scrub and a few hundred miles from pure desert.

Harrut had seen this type of heat wave once before, during his first fall in the city. The air had become dry in a way that he had previously associated with winter. Their lips cracked. Winds picked up from the east, peppering them with dust, and the sun brought the kind of heat that made wood buildings smell like they were about to catch fire.

But this time the meteorologists were wrong. The Arabs wore white headdresses, and the Europeans wore khaki suits with handkerchiefs shoved under their hatbands, but the heat wave never came.

Nevertheless, Harrut's work site remained closed due to union rules. It left him with no place to go, and by the third morning he was antsy. He woke a little after dawn, pulled the tea tin out from under his bed and counted the money. It was all there, of course. He cracked open Flori's door. "Wake up. Let's do something."

Flori was completely covered under her blanket, except for her arm. "You do something," she said from underneath. He watched her hand slide under the covers like a snake.

"We can go to the park."

"Harrut, it's far too early," she said.

"Far too early," he mumbled to himself. Through her window he watched sunlight pooling in the streets. "I'll teach you to swim."

"I know how to swim."

"Not very well." But he was secretly happy that she hadn't accepted his offer. Ever since his meeting with Sevag, he hadn't felt like going in the ocean. He considered calling Sirin but was worried about waking her parents, and beneath that was the worry that she would lecture him about Flori, that she would ask him more questions that he couldn't answer.

Instead he went to a local field, behind a row of leather shops, and watched some neighborhood youths play football. He recognized the young Syrian, the one he sold urchins to, as one of the players, and he was tempted to join the game, but they were only teenagers, so he just watched, hoping for an errant ball. When one finally came, he kicked it back to them in a graceful arc. "Good shot!" they yelled.

There were slush vendors on the street with glass-lined carts, so that people could see the whirling colored ice. The carts were relatively new to Beirut and still something of a novelty, so that they brought adults as well as children. Harrut had only tried the snowcones once, on a weekend stroll with Sirin. They'd bought an orange one and a green, but they were disappointed to find that both tasted the same. Harrut watched the carts go by and he drifted, forgetting himself. He followed a herd of pack animals, camels and mules. He watched the camels' expressions, how they perked up their ears and folded their nostrils against the wind. They reminded him of Parrig, and he resolved to visit Sirin before lunch.

They stood out on her front porch. She held Parrig like a baby, and the dog kept panting and snorting in Harrut's direction, licking at the endless stream of liquid snot running out of its nose.

"I think he has a cold," Sirin said.

"It's so warm, how could he get a cold? He probably has allergies."

"Well, I don't know. There he is—sick."

Harrut patted Parrig on the head a few times, careful to avoid being licked. A wave of disgust passed over him. He found himself very angry at the animal. He hated its wet nose and eyes. It was a calm and deep moment of hate, and it must have been primal, some biological thing. Then the anger moved to Sirin, or the way she held the dog, as though it was protection, something to keep him away. These emotions came and went in a few seconds.

He thought about the money under his bed, how Flori had surely found it and held it in her hands for just a moment before stuffing it back into the tea tin. Then, after they'd put Parrig inside, he took Sirin by the arm. They weren't going anywhere in particular, just walking. Harrut told the story of his day. He told her about the boys playing soccer and reminded her of how all ice slush tasted the same. And then, without really thinking, he invented a story about Sevag. He said that he had gone swimming and had nearly been run down by a boat sailed by a big fat man with a wooden leg. He made Sevag into a happy drunk who yelled long strings of obscenities toward the shore. By the end of the story, they'd both fallen out of the boat and were bobbing in the current. "Then a shark came," he said.

"You are a liar," said Sirin.

"And we gave the shark a drink too, so it got drunk and wouldn't eat us." He said this to make her laugh and, in a way, as an apology for the sudden, secret wave of spite that had come over him earlier.

"Terrible liar!" she grinned and shook her head.

But the next day, Harrut found that the same frustrations that had crawled up into his chest the previous morning had returned. Flori again refused to get out of bed. "After all the cooking I did for you," she said, for no reason that Harrut could see except to remind him of New York in a nasty way.

He fumed. "I may not cook, but I do a lot. I provide."

"But have you ever cooked or cleaned, Harrut? Do you know how to make dolmha?"

"I've seen mama make it so many times."

"But have you ever made it, by yourself? With your hands? No, you haven't. If you did, you would know what it's like."

"I do know."

"Then what is the first step?"

"To put the meat in the grape leaves."

"No, if you had ever made dolmha, you would know that the first step is to pick among the grape leaves; then you wash them."

"This is all very nice," he said.

"Then you lay them flat on a towel to soak up some of the moisture, and only after that do you start to put the rice in. Only then do you add the meat. So you don't know how to make dolmha, admit it."

Harrut said nothing.

"Why don't you admit it?"

"Big deal," he said. "I don't know how to make dolmha. I could learn. This has nothing to do with anything—you just want to fight."

"Yes, it does have to do with everything! You eat dolmha but you never make it. An ingrate like yourself should be happy to go to New York!"

"It has nothing to do with anything." But even Harrut, with his linear mind and sensibilities saw something in what she'd said. He wouldn't admit it, but he'd never cooked in his life. He'd never had to.

After the argument, he forced himself to shave which made him feel a little better, and headed off towards the beach. He couldn't imagine how he was going to make it through the week without work. He felt shabby and tense. He didn't go into the water but simply cast stones, seeing how many times he could skip them.

He carefully arranged a mental picture of arriving in New York, the same grey streets he'd seen in the black-and-white films that had played at his old movie theater. "My son, I am so happy you are here," his father would say. Then his father would kiss him, moving from one cheek to the other, and then adjust his light frame glasses and tie. He imagined a beige apartment on a cold day. The kitchen would be small but warm. The kitchen was his mother's domain, and she would never consent to live in a home with a cold kitchen. But in the other rooms, drafts would seep in through warped and cracked window casings. He flung his imagination further into the future, something he rarely did: he would go to school to learn English; he would get a job and slowly work his way up. Then one day his father would pull him aside, far in the future now. "My son," he would say, "we are going to move again." Where would they go? West, he imagined, always west.

The mental gymnastics, the process of imagining into a possible future, made him light-headed. He felt open to things in a way that he hadn't been for quite some time.

In front of him the waves churned and then seemed to cough up a young man. Harrut took a moment to recognize the swimmer, he was the young Syrian, the urchin dealer. The Syrian put in a few fierce strokes and then was able to stand and trudge up the beach. He walked right up to Harrut. "No work?"

Harrut took a moment to find his voice, "Still closed. Union rules."

The boy sat down near him, shifting around a moment to find a smooth spot among the rocks. "Why don't you go get me some urchins. That way you could make some money."

"I'm getting paid anyway," Harrut said.

The boy gestured out at the ocean again, and Harrut shook his head.

"Come on, Harrut. I saw you watching our game yesterday. I know you are not the type of person who likes to sit in one place. I'll race you."

Harrut threw another stone into the water without bothering to skip it. It fell in with a heavy thunk.

The Syrian shrugged his shoulders. He waded back into the water and then dove in. The young man was athletic and wiry, as good a swimmer as Harrut, probably not as strong but certainly faster. Harrut saw himself in Flori's role, watching a man swim out, getting smaller and smaller until all that was visible was a bobbing head and an occasional fan of sea spray. Harrut felt pins of jealousy- why couldn't he get in the water too? There was the sky and water, he reckoned, and the young man's head bobbing- nothing to be scared of. No reason came to him.

But what if Sevag hadn't been exaggerating? What if he had intended to drown himself that night? What if Flori was in his room, at that very moment, recounting the money under his bed? What if the heat wave finally came and burnt Beirut to fine char? What if sheep rose up and became a pagan army? What if he was alone? What if he was more like Don Quixote?

Without thinking, he looked around and picked up a grey rock. It was buttery to the touch and shaped as near to a disc as nature would allow. He threw it with a deft flick, watched it bounce, eight, nine, twelve times, the space between the bounces becoming so small that the stone seemed to be simply rolling on the water. He looked past the stone, mapping the trajectory it would follow if it could go forever, past the Syrian, past the horizon. And then he looked away. The stone would have sunk of course, although he didn't see it sink and therefore, there was the slimmest chance- at least in his own mind- that it was still rolling toward the horizon line.

He headed home to tell Flori. He was in a hurry to tell her because she would be happy.

Strength Training

To begin with, he was trying hard to be delicate with people. Armen was trying to do the right thing and be civilized, and that was the problem with the retarded kid, Elias Ekoski, who had a large head and told lies. He hated Elias a little more each day. The feeling had come loping up, real natural, like a stray dog that follows you down the street. Armen would watch Elias' head and think, *Big-headed retard.* Or- *This guy's head: it looks like an egg.* It was trouble.

He had promised Elias' parents it would be a good experience. He had promised Conway, the gym manager. Now here he was, disgusted, and these headaches he was having only gave him a short fuse. He wondered if, somehow, Elias wasn't the source of the headaches. "Sit up straight," he said again. "You're going to hurt your back."

"I'm getting stronger. Can't you tell?" Elias said. Another lie; the kid was as flabby and pale as ever. Armen was no shrink, but he could see by the knife-like edge in Elias' eyes that the boy was picking and sorting these lies, and they had little or nothing to do with his condition, ring chromosome 13 syndrome. What was a result of ring 13 was that Elias had an enlarged skull, bigger than usual, and it reminded Armen of the whosit aliens from *Star Trek*- the ones who also had giant ears. And he had some kind of mild retardation which was why his parents were paying extra to make sure Armen was always on hand. "Just in case," Mrs. Ekoski said, slipping Armen a cash tip before the first work-out. Mrs. Ekoski was a curvy, pink-skinned woman with baggy eyes that somehow matched her leather handbag, and she bit her lower lip when she watched her son handle weights.

"Come on. Keep your back straight, kid."

"Don't I look bigger?" Elias worked the barbells with a stiffness.

"Attaboy," Armen said, because he couldn't think of anything else.

"I'm gonna have big arms like you. I want to kick ass. Yesterday I won a fight at school."

"What do you know about fighting?"

"You gotta aim for the throat. Like Jet Li," Elias puffed as he hit his final rep.

Armen refused to look at him. Instead, he let his gaze wander over the chrome and black layout of the gym, Harold's 24-7, Hollywood.

"Do you know how to fight, Armen?"

"I was in AP for a while. I know something."

"AP stands for advanced placement. I'm in advanced placement."

"AP is a gang," Armen said.

"I'm going to be in a gang." He put the barbells down. "I'm going to have a bandanna, and tattoos, and a chrome ride." Was he being sarcastic or dead serious? Elias' voice, often a low-pitched monotone, gave little away.

"I think you've seen too many rap videos. There's no gang in your future." Armen continued quickly as a way of cutting off whatever else Elias was about to say. "I think you're on the road of straight and narrow. Just like me- get a job, do the right thing and you'll be okay. Now let's do the back machine."

He set Elias up at 40 pounds to start with, and there was a pretty woman to their right. She was running an ellipser. An iPod mini attached to her arm, she hunched forward slightly so that she could read a magazine.

Elias studied her. "She's leaning forward. You should tell her to stop, or she'll hurt her back."

"She's not my client. I'm working with you."

"I had sex with that girl," Elias said suddenly.

"Don't you wish."

"I did her up the ass."

"Hey, you watch it." Armen glanced over to make sure she hadn't heard. "You best watch your freaking mouth."

Elias took a moment to suck in a breath, his eyes screwed up in some adolescent look of defiance, and then he continued his reps.

"You fat fuckhead," Armen said under his breath so that Elias didn't hear. Armen felt tendrils of pain wrapping round his brain.

Right after he got home from the gym, he dialed up Justin, with whom he'd shared an apartment while getting his associates degree. Justin had his degree in computers and had gone on to a serious college.

"What's the story?" Justin said.

"Ring chromosome 13."

"Ring chromosome 13?"

"It's a genetic condition. Can it make people lie?"

"Armen, I'm in engineering, not some doctor."

"I need to know. There's this kid at the gym. He's making up all kinds of crap."

"Why don't you look it up on the internet?"

"We don't have internet. We were going to, but my roommates didn't want to split the bill. They say they'll never use it because they're almost never home"

"Fuck. I don't think a disease can make someone lie," Justin said.

"You don't think so?"

"I don't know, but I don't think so."

"I figured." Armen got off the phone and took stock of his marginally furnished room. A bed, particle-board shelving and a few unframed movie posters taped to the wall. A small TV planted in the corner. He turned on the ceiling fan and sat on the floor, leaning his head against the wall. He took in a series of long, quiet breaths.

This is what Armen did with his time: He woke at six,

went in early to the gym so he could get his own reps in. Most days, he focused on upper body, abs and back strength. Then, making use of that associates degree in physical therapy, he trained clients. He spent about 20 hours a week doing administrative or front desk duty and worked overtime when the chance came. He got a check on the first and fifteenth, paid his bills on time and gave a third of the rent money to Cyrus, one of his roommates. He took his ADD meds regularly. In the evenings, he usually played video games or watched TV with Danny, the other roommate. Sometimes he went out for a run or cooked a nicer than average dinner. About once a week, he called home and spoke with his mother.

When he lay down in bed, he often thought of women. He noticed them at the gym. Not that Armen went to work to stare at asses. It was more a product of the inevitable. If you were straight, he figured, and you worked at Harold's 24-7, you couldn't miss it. They wore small tops and tight shorts. Proliferation was the right word for it. A proliferation of the inevitable: pointy ankles, long, tight thighs, shorts wedged firmly between ass cheeks, exposed abdomens and navel rings. It wasn't that he regarded women as objects. He did not make inappropriate comments like Elias had, but sometimes he would project. He daydreamed about orgies. Naked women, flexing and then joining him in the steam room. Being sucked off in the shower. He was lonely. He was twenty five. He worked in a gym during the day and staved off boredom at night. Often, he cranked up the ceiling fan to block out the incessant LA heat and street noise. Then, near the edge of sleep, the headaches returned. Phantoms that left a dull, peripheral pain around the edges of his skull. They were more than a worry but not quite a threat. The type of pain that was there until he focused on it- even the thought of getting Tylenol sent it scurrying back to wherever it came from- only to return when he was occupied with something else.

His mother called. "Armen, when are you coming for dinner?" she asked in Armenian.

"I don't know."

"You have to tell me. So I can cook."

"I don't know. Sunday?"

"Sunday. Abris! Bravo!" she said. "How is your work?"

"Okay."

"Okay only, man? Yes? No?" She quipped in her joke-voice English that she used to make fun of him.

"It's fine Mama. I'll be there Sunday."

"Save your appetite. Are you sick? Are you still having headaches?"

"No Mama," he lied. "I just take aspirin. I'm fine."

"And you are still taking your special medicines?"

"Always."

Elias Ekoski kept showing for his twice-a-week, his mother smiling big and thanking Armen and once even showing her appreciation by cupping her manicured hands around his. Mr. Ekoski, on the rare occasions he came around, nodded mutely.

And Elias' list of lies continued to grow:

"I bought a Trans-am. It's cherry red with a dual-exhaust."

"I met Ozzy Osborne last night. At a coffee house in Beverly Hills."

"I'm going to start my own video game company."

"I fucked two girls at the same time."

"You have two cocks?" Armen asked. He wanted to hit him. Instead, he was good. He did his job, and whenever Elias was on a machine, Armen watched his big head tremble like a bobble-head doll.

Between the lies and the headaches, it was only a matter of time before disaster, and it finally came when Elias showed up wearing an extra big, blue bandanna, the type they sold for a dollar or two at Army surplus places. The bandanna was facing the wrong way, like Tupac Shakur used to wear, with the loose ends hanging around Elias' pale eyebrows. "I joined a gang," he said. Somehow, the whole get-up made Elias' skull look even larger and rounder, and Armen found himself speechless. He stood with his arms crossed, trying not to react. Finally he said, "Let's get you started with stretches."

Elias glared. "Did you hear me? I joined a gang."

Armen could feel heat rising in his chest. "No, you did not join a gang. You didn't. Where's your mom, Elias?"

"I told her to wait in the car!" His voice loud enough that

people stopped and stared.

"Listen, you little punk. Don't yell at me. You did not join a gang. I know about that shit. So you just keep your mouth shut." Armen could feel his cheeks and temples go red hot; he hadn't meant to sound quite so brutal.

Now the entire gym was watching, and Armen could see Conway, the manager, strolling over. Conway had broad shoulders and a confident walk. His hair was blond and cut in a step, and he was from Connecticut. He smiled professionally, "Armen? Everything alright? What's the problem? How are you Elias?"

"I'm good," said Elias. "Joined a gang."

"Armen," Conway said again and then gestured toward the back of the gym.

Armen gave Elias a black stare as he headed toward the office, and Elias nodded grimly back.

Conway fired him. Armen tried to explain. He admitted that it was an error in judgment on his part, and that he suffered from attention deficit disorder for which he took medications, and that he would be more aware around Elias in the future.

Conway nodded. He wished that they could work it out, he said, "However," he said, "I have to let you go. We have very clear policies in regard to customer service. You understand."

Armen told him: "Fuck you."

Conway somehow managed to keep his smile, but its gleam fizzled some.

"I'm through." Armen stood up. "It doesn't matter. There's a dozen other gyms around here, anyway. It really doesn't matter."

For years, Armen's mother had done him the favor of keeping the secret of his ADD from his father who regarded mental illness as a mark of shame, and that was one of the reasons Armen honored his Sunday lunches with her. He considered asking her to keep his firing a secret too, but watching his father brood at the other end of the dinner table, Armen knew there was only so much he could ask for. He would confess.

Timing his confession, he watched his father nibble at some moussaka. These days, his father was beginning to show his age and Armen sometimes found himself worrying. His father's eyes seemed to be a sinking into empty space beneath shaggy eyebrows. Was something wrong? Armen knew that topic couldn't be broached. Years before, he'd tried various abrupt tactics to get his father to open up, but they had only made for uncomfortable showdowns over dinner. So now he waited until things were quiet and everyone started to eat. Then he turned his attention to his younger brother, Raffi. His brother looked like some knock-off thug in his big jeans, Lakers jersey, and scraggly beard, but Armen was feeling better about Raffi these days. He realized that wannabee thuggery, like those messy clothes, was a phase that most people grew out of. Armen thought that he should spend more time with Raffi. They could shoot baskets or play video hockey at least. " Raff," he said. "Guess what? I got fired."

Raffi laughed with his mouth full, "You? Mister responsible guy got fired? Fuck!"

Their mother shot him a sharp look.

"Sorry Mama."

"Fired?" their mother said.

"It wasn't my fault, Mama. They had me training this kid. He's a sick kid. Sick in the head."

"So," she switched back to Armenian, "How can a sick boy make you lose your job?"

"Not sick like that. I mean, he's retarded."

"Ricky Retardo," said Raffi.

"He's missing some chromosome, I think," Armen tried to explain. "Like a gene, Mama. It's body chemistry."

"I know that."

"But he keeps lying."

"In Yerevan, we knew a boy who was sick in the head," his father said quietly without looking up. "The boy's name was Vartan. Sometimes, he would try to climb over the fence into our yard, to see the dog. When he saw the dog, he would get excited and laugh and spit would go down his chin. The dog would bark, so my brother and I would have to go outside and make Vartan leave. We threw sticks at him."

Armen tried to imagine the yapping dog, boys throwing sticks, and Vartan the village idiot and came up with a medieval picture of Yerevan, some crazy town of superstitious peasants, the mob in the old Frankenstein movies. He couldn't connect that primitive image with their lives: his father in his checkered golf shirt; Ikea furniture; and a large-screen TV at the far wall. Throwing sticks at retarded people? Had his ancestors come through some time warp? There was no place to sit the story of Vartan down at this dinner table, in this apartment, Hollywood, California.

"Why'd you throw sticks at him?" Raffi erupted.

"Parents of sick children should not let them out unsupervised. It's embarrassing for the community."

"But why didn't you just call his parents?" Armen asked.

His father regarded him with a hard-edged look. "You lost your job."

Armen thought better of answering directly, he didn't want to start an argument, and turned to his mother, "The problem is that this retarded kid, he lies all the time. It drove me crazy. I got mad at him and lost my job"

His mother pursed her lips. "Well, if he lies, then he cannot be sick in the head. Because you have to understand the nature of things in order to lie."

"She's got a point," Raffi added. "So whatcha gonna do, homeboy?"

"Find another job. Find one."

Armen was angry and nearly gave up on his ADD meds, but decided it would just make things worse, so he kept to them but questioned whether they were working. Maybe the pharmacy was accidentally giving him the wrong thing.

Mellow, he counseled himself. *Mellow man gets the job.* He got an interview for a trainer position at Club Health on Fairfax, but they offered him an aerobic instructor slot, and Armen told them he strictly did weights; he wasn't going to be bouncing and hopping in front of mirrors, and they said they would call him if a strength slot opened.

Mellow, he reminded himself, but compressed feelings came creeping up. They came at strange times. Playing video games on the X-Box, shopping for a new ball cap, talking with old friends from his gang days, and suddenly he would feel lost. He felt oversensitive and removed at the same time. Feelings jimjammed against each other, then came worrying, and then the quiet headaches. It pushed him to the point that he felt some relief at the distraction of opening the front door and finding Mrs. Ekoski standing there, looking big and somehow defensive in a navy business suit.

"Mrs. Ekoski."

"How are you Armen?"

"How did you find me?"

"I just asked the staff at the gym for your address," she said. "I hope you don't mind. I'd like to hire you back to start training with Elias again."

"I don't see how that could work." Armen stepped back to let her in.

"Wait," she said. "Listen, Elias refuses to do any sort of activity. He doesn't want to go to the gym. He hardly leaves the house. He says he won't exercise unless he has you back."

"He hates me."

"No, he just has a strong personality. Ever since he was little, Elias has derived a lot of self-esteem from being active. It engages him. He spent a lot of time playing with action figures, squirt guns and any kind of sport. All those things. Now, he mopes. Last week, he threw away his favorite Star Wars toys. And he got mad at me for asking why." Her eyes were a soft shade of bloodshot pink. Armen guessed that she was probably in her mid-40's, but he saw an almost childish vulnerability as well, as though she was made of fine crystal. He guessed that maybe this was what it was like to be a parent: to feel fragile.

"How old is he?" Armen asked.

"Probably too old for action figures now. He's made it abundantly clear that he would prefer to continue as your student."

"He's a liar."

"It's part of his condition."

"No it's not. I did some research on the ring 13 thing."

"Elias tells his stories as a coping strategy," she said. "He's an adolescent and has a hard time fitting in."

"He got me fired, and he'll get me fired again. He'll say something to tick me off. Do you know that, one time, he told me that he screwed some lady in the you-know-where while she was standing ten feet away? What if she heard?"

Mrs. Ekoski nodded soberly, but Armen could tell that she wasn't particularly surprised. "You know the odds of Elias ever finding a partner are pretty low. So he tells stories about sex; He's at that age. I've already spoken to him about the topic." And then, in a softer tone, she added, "Please."

He found himself suddenly aroused. Was it her body language, or maybe the memory of the pretty woman on the ellipser? Was it the way she'd said *please*? The feeling that they were both walking on pins? It seemed ridiculous, but there was some little thing passing between them. In some other life, he would cover her chin with his hand and lock into a shaky kiss. He would put his hand up against the back of her skirt. He felt that potential flutter. She was probably being neglected by Mr. Ekoski. The strain of caring for Elias had worn on their marriage. What was the husband's name? Bob? Bob rarely showed up at Elias' sessions, and when he did, he scowled and hardly spoke. "Okay," he said. "So, give me something I can work with."

"You can train him at our home," she said. "We have a garage space that we turned into a home gym. There will be no boss to fire you. You'll be the boss. We'll pay you as much as we paid at Harold's."

Armen nodded.

"Thank you," she said. She gave her phone number and address, and that was that.

He watched her go. "One more thing. Take off your clothes and let me bang you hard," he said after he'd closed the door, so she couldn't hear him. He sighed loudly enough that he could hear the echo bouncing off the bare walls.

He had almost a week to get through before he would go

to the suburbs, Agoura Hills, and start training Elias again. He passed the time playing video games, applying for other jobs and fending off edges of headaches.

After a few days of this, he decided to pay Raffi a visit. Maybe they'd shoot some baskets, but Raffi wasn't home. "I think he's at the store, helping your father," his mother said. "Are you hungry? You look tired, Armen."

"I'm okay, Mama." He got back into his car and drove to the grocery that his father had run for nearly three decades. He hadn't been to the shop in years. From outside, it seemed run down. The stucco facade was worn and dotted with paint splotches to hide graffiti and gang tags. *Yerevan Grocer, Armenian and American Grocery Product,* the sign, backlit in amber, had a representation of a craggy mountain behind the silhouette of a village.

Through the plate glass window, he could see his father standing, motionless, at the register. He knew that if he walked in, his father would offer him some halvah or sesame candy. His father didn't look like much. A stooped build, square shoulders, cheeks hollowing, flat hair and eyebrows ready to explode. Was this really the man he'd been so angry at for so many years? Or was this just some random, sad-eyed ethnic grocer? He tried to guess what his father might be thinking about. Possibly a new produce order. Maybe about his wife, or about car payments. Or about something that had happened long ago- throwing sticks at a retarded boy in Yerevan. The medieval images returned as he opened the door.

"Armen," his father said.

"I'm looking for Raff. Is he working?"

"He was here earlier, but then he went. Do you want halvah?" His father cut an ample piece, wrapped it in wax paper and handed it over the smudged counter top.

Armen ate in silence for a few moments. Finally, he said, "Did you have halvah like this back in Yerevan?" His father considered, then turned to dusting some canned goods. "No, the halvah here is imported and too dry. I liked it better at home."

"Why did you throw sticks at the retarded boy?" The question had slipped out. He hadn't planned to ask.

"That's just what we did. People were more straightforward back then. People were mean, but this was accepted." He faltered for a moment, then switched to Armenian. "Meanness was understood, let me explain, because being mean was what we knew. And it was clear. If a teacher hit your hand with his ruler, then you learned to sit quietly. If the police hit you with their clubs, you learned that crime was wrong. It was how things were made clear. Not just in Yerevan, but all over the world. It was only recently that everyone decided that it was wrong to hit and be mean. The world is softer now." These were probably the most words his father had strung together in years, and his face had gone slightly red. Then he added, "I think your brother went to the movies with some friends," and the subject seemed closed. The blush slowly left his face as he pulled a broom from the closet. "I have to sweep the floor.

Will you watch the register?"

Armen nodded. He noted that the halvah was sweet but also dry, as his father had suggested. He stood quietly at the register and watched as his father methodically swept each aisle.

As he passed from one hill to the next, the heat and noise of the city dissipated. Agoura was clean and cool, and the roads wound like question marks. Elias was in the front yard, wearing his wannabe bandanna. "It's you!" he yelled.

"You ready to work-out Elias?"

In a grassy slope, the yard led up to the massive Ekoski home, and Mrs. Ekoski watched them from up there, through an open patio door. "Show Armen the garage!" she called out. "Show him where we set up the weight bench."

Elias ignored her. "I want to be in a gang."

Mrs. Ekoski came down to them. "I'm happy you came," she said to Armen. She was wearing a sweater and snug jeans.

"Hi, Mrs. Ekoski."

"Call me Barbara, please."

"Call her Barbara, please," Elias said.

She stared at her son for a moment, then turned back to Armen. "Would you like the tour? Elias, why don't you wait in the garage? You can start to stretch or whatever you need to do."

The lot was three acres, she told him. A stone path led up

to the house, a two-story, stucco compound with windows and patio doors everywhere. Inside, it was cool, with mostly tile floors, and strangely empty like a museum. Barbara Ekoski would occasionally say something about architecture to him, and he would nod. Now and then as they walked, he stole a glance at her ass.

They exited through a rear slider and arrived at a large pool set in a brick courtyard. A shirtless young man, angular and decked out with half a dozen tattoos, worked a skimmer, siphoning brown leaves from the water. "Hey Barbara," the young man said.

She introduced him as Eddy Lopez, the pool guy, and Armen regarded him warily from across the shimmering pool.

"Elias likes to swim sometimes," she offered. "You could have him do some laps if you think it's okay."

"Is he your only child?"

She nodded. "Just one. What about you?"

"I don't have no kids. I have a brother."

"Do you get along? That's nice." She walked him back through an airy kitchen laid out with wreaths of dried chili peppers. Bob Ekoski was at the table with a laptop, and he started suddenly when they walked in.

Barbara Ekoski made a soft, apologetic noise. The two regarded each other for a moment.

"This is the guy from the gym?"

"This is Armen."

"Hey Mr. Ekoski. Nice to see you again."

Bob shuffled his fingers over his keyboard. "You're here to work with Elias, right? I mean, you're going to go and work out with him?"

"Oh," Barbara Ekoski said. "I'm just giving him the ten-cent tour. Maybe they'll use the pool to swim laps."

Bob took his glasses off, rubbed at his watery eyes. "I didn't mean to be rude. I've been stressed. The car is acting funny. They expect me in Santa Barbara in the morning."

She gently took a hold of her husband's shoulder while Armen stood awkwardly. He wasn't sure exactly what to do while the Ekoskis discussed their car problems, and then switched to the topic of a grocery list and, finally, how they could wire their entertainment system in some special way, and they seemed to have forgotten him. "Well," he said, "I better go out and see Elias. The garage is this way?"

The Ekoskis both apologized for seeming distracted, they were just a bit overwhelmed at this point, and they hoped he could understand. Barbara Ekoski sent him back to the front patio door.

Sitting on the weight bench in the garage, Elias wore a sour little expression.

Armen regarded him for a moment. "A gang, huh?"

Elias nodded.

"Well we got to whip you into shape then. Nobody'll let you in a gang unless you get big."

"I am big."

"How about some upper body today?"

Elias went through his reps in an awkward, withdrawn manner and finally, when he was finished, he said, "You like my mother."

"She's a nice lady. I don't like her like that, if that's what you mean."

"You want to have sex with her, I mean." Elias stared.

He grabbed Elias by his sweaty collar and held him long enough to see fear in the boy's eyes. "If you don't shut up," he whispered, "I'll fucking kill you."

Elias' eyes were blue explosions, but he shut up.

And Armen felt as though someone had run electricity through his chest. Without another word, without going inside to collect his first paycheck, he walked in a straight line to his car. Probably because of that feeling, a wave of adrenaline making him extra aware, he noticed Barabara Ekoski watching them, Elias and him, through a small-sized window on the second floor. How long had she been there, staring? Was that what had triggered Elias' comment? Her face close up to the window pane, she stared as though she might be in a trance.

Elias followed Armen's gaze up to the window and casually waved to his mother. That broke the trance, and she waved down at them, but Armen pretended not to notice. He closed the car door and drove fast.

He needed the money, so he went back twice a week for Wednesdays and Saturdays. He was careful to avoid direct eye contact with Barbara Ekoski and only spoke to answer her questions. He swore to himself that he would leave if Elias embarrassed him in front of her, but Elias, maybe sensing this, didn't say anything out of the ordinary. In fact, Elias let Armen drive him hard, to the point that Elias was breaking heavy sweats, and an etch of muscle tone was starting to show on his arms and legs. That's how it went, both of them training in spooky quiet. Sometimes with sounds of Eddy Lopez working at the pool, and sometimes with Barbara Ekoski watching them from her window. Maybe she was worried about her son, Armen reasoned, but it ate away at him, to the point that he had a dream that he was standing in the Ekoski house, in her place, looking out and, somehow, watching himself and Elias. In the dream, he saw himself putting Elias through some strange ritual, an initiation to a fantastic cult of shadowy consequence.

It was the week of the dream that Armen finally caught up with his brother. He convinced Raffi to play ball at a local park. But things got nasty. Armen fell behind, he couldn't get anything through the net, and he started roughhousing, throwing elbows. Then Raffi shoved him back, and Armen wound up throwing the ball at his brother's face. Armen paced the entire circle of the court before he came back and apologized.

Raffi held his pointer finger over a trickle of blood flowing from his left nostril. "What's your problem, man?"

"I'm sorry, I said."

"What's your fucking problem, Armen?"

"Nothing."

"You've been acting weird since you lost your job."

Armen dribbled the ball slowly, letting it bounce off the blacktop with fat, rubber smacks. "Why do people lie, Raff?"

"Oh shit! You're still going on about that Ricky Retardo kid?"

"Seriously Raff. Why do people tell stories? What's the point?"

"You're asking me? You're older." Raffi wiped away some more blood onto his oversize jersey. "I dunno. Why does anyone lie? Because they want something, I guess. Or to protect themselves. I remember you telling some crazy-ass lies yourself, bro. What does this retarded kid want?"

"Don't know."

"Why don't you ask him?"

"I'm not going to ask him. Fuck him. We should get some ice for your nose. I'm not going to worry about it."

"I think you're already worried about it ."

"I'm not going to worry."

But it was too late for that. The next time he went to Agoura, he felt nothing but dread. He pulled into the driveway and realized nothing was going to change. Elias was still grim and moody. His tattoos baking in the sun, Eddy Lopez was perpetually cleaning the pool, and looking out on all of them was Barbara Ekoski. And as for Armen, he needed the money. Job hunting wasn't as easy as he thought. He came to realize that checking the box that read: *do not contact my former employer* was hurting his chances. He was trapped. His headache flared with vengeance.

"I stretched already," Elias said as he got out of the car. He had his bandanna on tight.

"Don't you ever take that thing off?"

"When I sleep."

"Take it off now."

"No."

"You need to wash it. It looks dirty, kid."

"No."

"What do you want?"

Elias squinted.

"What the fuck do you want from me?"

The boy froze for a moment. Armen suspected there were all sorts of answers wrestling in the boy's head. "I want to be known," he finally said in a clear and thoughtful tone. "I want people to know who I am."

"So you made up some story about joining a gang because you think that means people will want to know you?"

Somehow, she must have sensed trouble because Barbara Ekoski was walking out of the house toward them.

Armen saw her. He was running out of time. "You know what you got to do if you want to be in a gang."

"What?"

"Come on, Elias. You know. You've seen it in a hundred movies. Gang initiation."

"Get your ass kicked?"

"Get your ass kicked," Armen nodded. "So come on. Take a swing. And hurry, you're mom's coming."

He didn't move.

"Come on kid."

"I can't."

"Now or never. Your mom's coming."

And like that, Elias hit him. Jabbed him really, and then Armen hit him back. Armen willed his fingers into a fist. He'd tried so hard to be good, but here he was. For the first time, he did not notice Elias' big head. Instead, he focused on Elias' fragile, blue eyes. Blue eyes like glass. He wasn't going to hit Elias very hard. In fact, he hit him hardly at all, just enough to give him an adrenaline rush: the start of the shakes; heart pounding; breath trapped firmly in his lungs. After that blow, Armen knew, Elias would feel strangely awake and probably more alert than he ever had. It would frighten his mother. And Armen, his head clearing, would have to find another job.

The Rat King

The Rat King first appeared in The King's English

It was him. For a moment, Aram guessed that it might be an ugly, very ugly, man or someone in costume maybe, but Aram used a finger to push his glasses up and get a better view, and it was him, no doubt. He panicked. His legs tensed, and he swallowed so hard that he nearly choked. If he hadn't already been anxious and groggy, it might have been too much. Or, it occurred to him, maybe it was because he felt this way that he was able to see the Rat King. Maybe this was the time to see.

The Rat King sat down next to him. Aram was surprised that neither attendant was in the room; he remembered that one had gone out for coffee, and he wasn't sure where the other was. Besides Sevart there were five other patients, four of whom were asleep- it was just before seven in the morning- and the fifth wore oversize headphones, watching some movie on her portable DVD, and if she saw the Rat King, she gave no indication.

The Rat King looked at Sevart, who was dozing in a haze of Benadryl and uremic symptoms. "Your wife is sick," he said. His voice was guttural and harsh, but also layered over with a mousy squeak that seemed appropriate for a rodent type.

Aram's jaw remained stuck. He stared. He closed his eyes tight, opened them again.

"Aren't you going to say *hello*?" The King extended a naked, pink paw. In the Rat King's way, the paw was human and animal. Rodent, man, and demon, and it was difficult to see where one part ended and the other began. That's how it was with him.

Aram did not take his paw. Instead, he looked again at the dialysis patient with the DVD player, confirmed that she had taken no notice of a six foot tall rat-man dressed in office attire. This was a stress dream, a symptom of the strange feelings and urges that had been coming over him lately, and if he waited long enough, the Rat King would simply fade back to wherever he'd come from. Aram sat still for almost a minute, not daring to look directly at the grizzled figure to his left. It had been decades since they'd been this close together, and he'd forgotten how creepy the King could be; his beady, blank eyes, the unnerving rodent head stuck on a humanoid body, the proportionately too-small hand-things. The smell- chalk, sulfur and rotten fruit. Aram's skin crawled. His throat spasmed with vomit reflex. Finally, he let himself see his own reflection in the Rat King's eyeballs. "You're not real," Aram said.

The Rat King shrugged. "Neither is God, but that doesn't stop Him from causing all sorts of trouble. So, can I get you a cup of coffee?"

Aram shook his head.

"All right then. I'll just sit with you. How's your wife?"

Sevart looked pale. She'd painted her lips red before they'd left the house, and they stood in contrast to her white face. He watched her breathe. He thought that the issue of God's existence might be up for debate, but the Rat King was right in that He did cause all sorts of trouble. In this case, the trouble manifested in the dark line of blood rising from Sevart's scar-like fistula, into tubes, to the artificial kidney and back down again. It noiselessly completed its circuit, clean now. Maybe it was his imagination, but he thought her fingers and hands looked slimmer and less puffy.

When he again screwed up enough courage to turn and look, the Rat King was gone, but there was a cup of black coffee thoughtfully propped up on the chair in such a way that it would be difficult to spill.

"Were you talking to a man?" Sevart reached gingerly under the cab seat for her bag.

"A man?"

"Yes- Careful Aram, my legs are still tired." She put her arm over his as he paid the driver.

She did look better, Aram had to admit. He figured this all might work: the special diet, the dialysis sessions, good habits, pills and treatments. It was his background in engineering- he'd always thought of his marriage as some sort of marvelous engine- and, when there were problems, they would adjust the engine, tinker with various solutions to get it running smoothly again. Sometimes, he'd learned, the solution was just time. Sometimes it was extra maintenance. But, with big issues like when Lori was born, the death of their parents, diabetes and kidney failure, the machine would require significant overhaul. The heart of the engine might have to be replaced entirely, and then the problem became how to fuel the change. When they were younger, they could fuel on adrenaline, coffee and sweets. As they got older, they burned money, maybe a bank loan. But now they were retired, living on what amounted to fixed income. Sevart wasn't really allowed sweets, and she couldn't drink coffee after two. Aram often felt spent. Nevertheless, he hoped that some miracle might still let the engine come through.

"What are you thinking about?" She looked at him.

"I'm happy because the dialysis seems to have helped. You look healthier, Sevart, and thinner already."

"It's all about thinness with you men!" But he knew that she was teasing him.

"I mean the swelling!"

"I feel lighter," she said. "We have to tell Lori. She'll be happy."

They were halfway up the stairs to their unit when she asked again, "Who was the man?"

"Which man, Sevart?"

"You were talking to a man in the kidney room. He was big and very hairy. He had a blue tie."

"There was no one."

"I saw. I thought I saw."

"You were asleep the whole time." He unlocked their door. "That must have been a dream."

The sun was on its way down. He regarded the phone as though it was a trap. From a practical perspective, he appreciated the idea of a telephonic system, how it allowed for prompt delivery of information, how lives might be saved by dialing 911, but beyond that he'd never liked the way it compelled people to try to fill empty time with words. He'd never been a big talker. And who would he call, anyway? There was Melbourne, of course, but he knew that his suppers with Melbourne worked precisely because neither of them brought emotional baggage, just two old engineers swapping stories, and he may have been a modern parent in some ways, but he'd never feel comfortable telling his troubles to Lori, who had a prickly disposition to begin with. There was no one. Even his conversations with Sevart had become sparse. What was there to talk about? Of the kidney failure, it seemed as though everything had been said. They didn't have a child at home anymore, nor grandchildren. They had no work to talk about, and old friends had died or were dying or had moved to the far suburbs.

He couldn't hear a sound from the bedroom. Sevart might have been sketching with her pastels, a hobby she'd taken up after the diagnosis. But more likely, she was asleep. When they'd first found out, he'd asked her to consider exercise, taking walks, and even suggested they buy a stationary bike, and she'd gone along with the plan. Sevart had said that she was going to conquer her condition. She said they would be out dancing and living life to its fullest, but when she was active, she became thirsty, and she was on a fluid-restricted diet. So now she sketched or slept, and the house stayed quiet.

So he sat and stared at the phone with its tiny green light. Shadows crept up the walls. For some reason, modern designers loved to affix tiny LED lights to things, and he took a few moments to contemplate his living room: the blinking pins on the smoke detector, the green one on the phone and another two on the caller ID box, the orange one that indicated that the fancy new vacuum cleaner was recharging, one-two-three on their VCR, more on the big TV. He remembered that, not so long ago, dark had been darker, more clean and complete.

He picked up the phone - these new phones had all kinds of features- and hit the intercom button. "Hello," Sevart's voice was even as always but tired.

"It's me."

"Where are you, Aram?"

"In the living room."

"Are you joking? Why don't you just come in and talk to me?"

"The last time I did, you got angry."

She groaned softly. "I'm sick. You know I didn't mean anything that time."

"Do you need anything?"

"No, thank you. You do know that I didn't mean anything that time - right?"

"Oh, yes."

"I'm sick," she said emphatically. "Sick people get angry sometimes for no explainable reason. You're an educated man, Aram, you must understand that."

"I do," he said. "I will come in and kiss you goodnight then."

"I would like that very much." She hung up.

He walked into the bedroom and kissed her gently. Her sketch pad lay on the bed, opened to a half-finished work. She had drawn a landscape, terraced hills, and above flew strange looking birds.

She held onto his hand for a moment, and he let his other hand stray to her breast, but she just laughed in an uncomfortable way, and he took it back. "What are those? Birds?" he asked as a way of deflecting the awkwardness of the moment.

"Birds?"

"In the drawing." He pointed to her sketch pad. As he leaned closer, he saw that the creatures had bird bodies but fantastical heads. Some had reptilian heads. Others seemed to have doglike heads, and a few had human heads. The human heads, as Sevart drew them, were simple and done in bold strokes with exaggerated features like characters in political cartoons.

"I just draw things to suit my fancy," she said. She picked up the sketch pad, knocking her pastel crayons to the floor and closed it so he could no longer see. "I just do it for fun."

"It's interesting," he said.

"Maybe I'll show you when I'm done." She gave him a small kiss on the cheek. "But I'm sleepy now, Aram."

When he went back into the living room, he pushed the massive TV aside so he could unplug all of their video components. He unplugged the vacuum; it was probably charged anyway. He went into his tool bag and used electrician's tape to cover up all the other little lights, one by one, until the only one left was the smoke detector, which he knew he couldn't cover. He looked up at it, and it blinked back at him in a manner that suggested it had some sliver of personality, as though it was somehow flirting with or teasing him, and he found himself more frustrated and angry than he'd been in a long time.

The next time with the Rat King was when he was walking through the Russian section of Allston. The tiny delis and stern old men in hats and scarves reminded Aram of his father. He was turning the corner near the Gorky Bookstore, which displayed stuffed roosters in its window, when he realized that he was being followed.

"It's ironic that I should find you here." The Rat King spread his arms to indicate the entire neighborhood. "In the Russian ghetto! That's where we met, no? Tchaikovsky, remember?"

He did remember. It had been his first year in the United States when his parents had taken him to see *The Nutcracker Suite*. The second half, the international dances and set-pieces, he could have done without, but the first act had pulled him in and, as it was for many little boys, the most compelling scene was the battle between the Nutcracker and Rat King. There was something otherworldly about how the dancer inside the bulky Rat King suit had moved. On the way home, Aram had recounted the story to his parents. "Remember the dancing bear?" he'd asked in Armenian. "Remember the soldiers? Remember the Rat King?"

"It was wonderful," his mother said.

"I didn't like the second part. Nothing happened."

"They were dancing, and the girl and the Nutcracker were watching the dances from their thrones," his mother reminded him.

"But nobody fought!" and that night, in his dreams, he met the Rat King for the first time.

Aram walked faster past the stuffed roosters, but the Rat King kept up, step for step. There were plenty of people on the sidewalk, but none of them looked at the King; neither did anyone walk into him. People simply veered, without prompting, to the right or to the left.

Then the Rat King touched him. Reached right over and grabbed Aram's arm. Everything - the hard tug at his elbow, the pressure of the King's well-manicured claws - felt perfectly real. "When I'm talking to you, look at me. Unless you would like to get into a fight, right here, on this sidewalk, you'd best look at me."

"I've beaten you in every fight that mattered," said Aram, but he did turn to face the King. If anything, the Rat King, like Aram himself, looked old. He had grown a bit of a paunch, a fatty jowl under his rodent chin, and some of his whiskers had gone grey. Aram thought, although he couldn't quite confirm, that the King's eyes were redder and more baggy than they had been before - the look of a man, or creature, who hadn't slept well in some time. He nodded to the Rat King. "So, do you have children?"

The Rat King's laugh bordered on braying, and a passing group of college kids looked around, possibly baffled by a sound they couldn't quite hear or place. "I have a hundred children! More! I'm a rat."

Aram nodded soberly. "I have one daughter. She's difficult sometimes. She wants, I think, more than she should. But how can you ever tell your children that?"

The King nodded. "I've had to kill a few of mine, Aram. It's never easy. What is your daughter's name?"

"I don't think I'll be telling you."

"I understand," the Rat King fixed the top button on Aram's black coat. "Well, I'm here to help you. I want to help in your time of trouble."

"No." Aram turned around and headed back toward his home.

"You are extremely ungrateful, Aram. The least you can do is listen to me, especially in light of all the times that you killed me."

"Those were a child's fantasies." Aram tried to keep his voice from straining.

"It was real enough for me." The Rat King huffed to keep up with him, which was nice, because it meant that Aram wasn't the only one who'd fallen out of shape. "Remember the duel we fought on the glacier top in the Bering Strait? Do you know how much it hurt when you gutted me with that harpoon? Not to mention the time you pushed me into the vat of boiling oil. It took me weeks to even be able to talk afterward; the pain was traumatizing."

A homeless man with a long grey beard - Aram recognized him from previous walks - held a coffee cup out toward them. "What you neglected to mention," Aram said, "was that you had it coming each time. When we fought on the glacier, how close were you to pushing a pitch-fork right through my face?"

"I don't know," answered the homeless man. "But if you give me a dollar, I might remember."

Aram dug into his pockets but didn't find any change, and he'd left his wallet at home as a matter of habit. "I'm sorry," he told the homeless man.

"Me too." The man turned and held his cup out to passing group of Russian matriarchs.

"Listen!" the Rat King hissed. "Listen, it was you who were the killer. You killed me so many goddamned times. All that pain, you couldn't imagine. And what was the worst injury you sustained? A bruise? A scraped knee?"

"I broke my arm."

"That was from playing soccer. Not from me."

"I was a child! Does that answer your question? If I had died, it would have been forever. You - you're immortal."

"No, an immortal never dies, Aram. I am very much mortal. The only difference was that, after I died, I was brought back to life again. The cycle began anew."

"Well, what kept bringing you back, then?"

The Rat King grinned in a sharp way. Something in his expression, Aram couldn't explain what, suggested sympathy. "Aram, you are smart fellow. I know. I've peeked into your life over the years. Remember when you were in engineering school? You prided yourself on being intelligent. You were a scholar, a man of games and puzzles. If you don't know who kept bringing me back to life, if you can't figure even that out, then your mind has dulled considerably."

As the Rat King's breath rose in white mist, Aram bit his lower lip and sighed.

The Rat King gently took Aram's right hand and put a scrap of paper into his palm. "Meet me at this address, just outside the building, Thursday night at nine. I doubt that your wife will notice that you are gone, but if she does see you leave, just say that you are going to market." The Rat King, careful so that his surgical-sharp nails didn't go through Aram's gloves, curled Aram's hand into a fist and began to walk away.

"Wait," Aram said. He unfolded the paper. *Twelve Latham Way.* "What is this?"

"A place of ill repute," the Rat King sang back to him as he disappeared around a corner.

This boy who'd been so fascinated with the Rat King, he'd been an imaginative child, a tinkerer, an engineer-in-waiting, and he'd spent nights mapping an elaborate fantasy world in his head. His fantasy world simulated the real one, but on a mythic scale. His Himalayas were taller, colder, more pure. His Mariana Trench- he was the type of child who knew all about the Mariana Trench- was deeper and more sinister. Atlantis lay just below the waterline. And all these locations served as exotic backdrops for the endless duel: He and the Rat King. They fought on mountaintops and on the backs of camels. They fought atop the Empire State Building and in the Taj Mahal. A desperate race to stop the Rat King's conspiracies: bombs big enough to destroy the earth, kraken-like sea monsters, armies of shadowy rat-men to do his bidding. In those years, he'd closed his eyes, created this life, fought the endless battle. And at night his dreams picked up where his imagination left off.

He'd rarely cooked for Sevart before, but it was now becoming common. Safe things: roast beef wrapped in cabbage with a side of fresh spinach salad, a special dressing, and her ration of water. Water was an issue. Sevart was a chubby woman, not big but certainly round, and before the illness, she was used to having her way with drinks and treats. And now he poured her eight-ounce glasses with care, using a small chalkboard they'd hung in the kitchen to tick off the ounces.

She watched him pour and then said, "Some more, Aram. A little more."

"We should leave extra water for later," he said. "You know how your throat gets dry at night." The water, such a piddling amount. He couldn't think of anything comforting to say that he hadn't said before, so he gently cupped his hands around the back of her neck.

On the table was her drawing pad. She'd begun a new work. It was still sketchy, but he easily recognized two people standing side-by-side. Was this supposed to be Sevart and him? Did they look old? They might've. She'd used mostly grey in drawing their flesh and given them masklike features. Did they look like the painting, *American Gothic*, lost and isolated? Maybe. These two people seemed to be standing inside or underneath something. A cave? A vast grey umbrella? He couldn't quite tell. He didn't ask.

He went back to preparing the roast beef. It was nearly done, and for no reason, he thought of the address. He'd thrown it right out, crumpled it up and tossed in the first trash can he'd seen. But, of course, he'd already memorized it: *Twelve Latham Way*. He was old, but not too old to have urges. It had been a long time, more than six months, since Sevart had shown even a passing interest, and now: *Twelve Latham Way*. No place he'd ever heard of. Some side street.

He imagined a red bed. A firm, young ass, buoyant breasts and long brown hair. *Twelve Latham Way* wore a silky, pink negligee.

"I think I hear someone," Sevart told him. "Coming up the stairs."

Who? The Rat King? A woman in a pink negligee? His mind spun until he could fix on the urgent clomp of Lori's boots.

Sevart was suddenly smiling, headed for the door.

Lori wore a big red coat against the cold. Her hair, dyed blond these days, was wet, and she carried a canvas bag. She kissed them each on the cheek and shoved the bag, which was full of fruit, into Aram's hands. "These are the fruit. Remember the doctor said? I got peaches! Apples!"

Aram nodded. He was anxious during Lori's visits because he often found himself ruffling her feathers by accident.

"Oh Mom, you look terrible!" Lori looked back at him. "She looks so tired."

"How are you, Lori?"

"Did you use those aroma therapy sticks that I got you?"

"The vanilla and creams? They were very nice," Sevart lied.

"Good. I'll order you some more. And it's important for you to moisturize your skin. Remember, we saw it on the web site? And if there's anything - anything at all - you can always ask me." Lori spoke quickly, as though she upset in some way that Aram couldn't quite place.

"Well," Aram tried, "it's nice to see you here. We were sitting down for dinner. Do you want to eat?"

"I ate." She waved him off. He was hopeless.

Both he and Sevart had been quiet, laid-back people, one of the secrets of their long-term marital success. So was Lori's manic energy a form of rebellion? She'd been this way since she'd turned thirteen. After college, she'd harnessed that energy and turned it into a career in advertising, a field in which her personality seemed to pay off. She went to the gym each night, was perpetually single and, especially since Sevart's renal failure, increasingly critical of Aram, who watched her as she pulled Sevart out of their kitchen. "I'm going to inspect what you've done to the bedroom," she hollered at him from down the hall. "Did you buy that memory foam mattress like I said?"

He watched them until the swinging kitchen door closed, blocking his view. He heard Lori talking to Sevart, exclaiming loudly in the bedroom now. He prepared a dinner plate for himself, and one for Sevart. Then he prepared a third plate for Lori, thought better of it - he might be scolded - and put her food back. He sat and picked at his spinach as he waited for his wife to be returned.

The next few days, he was extremely nervous. But nervousness, paradoxically, gave him a cloak of normalcy. It kept him locked in safe routines. He washed dishes, took out the trash, watched his regular TV shows with Sevart, and called Melbourne to set up their next night out. He took

Sevart to her appointments, filled out the new Medicare plan forms, and vacuumed every other day. He silently rehearsed the lie like a schoolboy memorizing lines for a play.

But in the end, he did not need the lie. Sevart was in a deep sleep when he left their apartment. He took a cab across the river to a part of Cambridge he'd never seen before. True to his word, the Rat King was waiting. "You're late. It's a good thing I factored that into my plans. She's in 14B." The King slid two hundred dollars into Aram's hand. "She is lovely, or so I've heard. She described herself over the telephone machine as having firm, round thighs."

Aram was a moral man. He paid his taxes and obeyed laws; the type of man who followed rules that others considered silly or intrusive. He understood that societies prospered because they were built on order, but this time he let his feet lead him across beat-up tile floors, to the elevator. The Rat King had exaggerated - not a big surprise - in that this wasn't a bordello but an old apartment house with a tiny elevator that must have been a relic of the 1930's. *I have immoral feet*, Aram thought, *immoral hands*. He knocked at the door.

She opened it a crack, as much as the security chain would allow, enough for him to see her face, a bit of a white silk robe, some prominently displayed cleavage. Her face was round and pretty with soft skin. She reminded him of cream. His cock stiffened just a little in that way that can be uncomfortable for men in public, although he took with it a small measure of relief since he didn't always get good performance from it.

"Who are you?" she said.

"I have two hundred dollars." He rolled the bills tightly and pushed them through the space in the door.

She took the money and the door slammed shut and, just for a second, Aram realized that he was alone, completely. He realized his situation, all his situations: Sevart's quiet disease; his inability to connect with Lori; the return of an imaginary childhood foe; the layered ennui of grandchildless retirement years; the fact that he was suddenly willing to make use of the services of a prostitute. No one knew where he was, and what if something happened? He considered bolting as she reopened the door.

Throughout their encounter, he'd felt light-headed, and if someone had told Aram that he had just put on a condom for the first time in his life and stumblingly, haltingly gone through intercourse with this girl, this Kelly, he would not have questioned that description, but he also would not have quite been able to recall it either. It took him less than three minutes to come. He did remember being grateful that Kelly appeared much younger than Lori. Being with a woman his daughter's age would have been humiliating. Being with one who looked even younger was simply surreal. Later, he would remember Kelly's breasts. They reminded him of golden medallions, or twin bulbs from a Christmas tree perhaps. They were something he'd somehow won.

She stayed in bed, naked with one leg crossed over the other. "Do you like vodka?"

"No, thank you." Aram rubbed at his eyes, found his glasses and put them on. He knew full well how ridiculous he looked wearing only them, but the room was dimly lit, and he would never be able to locate his pants otherwise. He turned to find himself at a window that faced the street. Far below, a shadowy figure regarded him from under a street lamp and gave some sort of hand signal. Aram snapped the curtains shut.

"Why did you close those curtains?" Kelly was suddenly up, sliding on blue jeans.

"I'm sorry." Aram took a hesitant step back. "I just realized I was naked for all the world to see." He found his pants. "I will open them again if you like."

"Don't do that again," she said. "Besides, no one can see us up here."

"Maybe somebody can."

"They'd have to have really good eyes. You have some kind of accent. Are you Russian?"

"I was born in Armenia, but we moved when I was very young."

"I'm Russian," she said. "That's why I said if you liked vodka. It was like a test."

"You have no accent at all."

Not looking at him, she continued to dress, and he thought, yes, she could be Russian. The round face and the blue eyes. "But a Russian named Kelly?"

"Don't be stupid. That's not my real name."

"Then what?"

"I'm not going to tell you my real name anymore than you're going to tell me yours."

"You can call me the Rat King if you like," Aram said.

She squinted back at him. "I hate rats. They're disgusting."

"It wasn't my choice."

"Well, get a better name next time." She unlatched and opened the door so that he might leave, and as he stepped out, she shoved a small bottle of vodka under his arms. "Vashe zdorovye," she said with a sharp Russian accent.

"Genats," he said softly to her in Armenian.

He handed the bottle off to the Rat King when he got back onto the street.

"How did you like her, Aram?"

"She was nice."

"That's all?"

"What more do you need?"

"I paid," the Rat King hissed as he shoved the bottle back into Aram's coat. "I deserve to know. Did she take you in her mouth?"

"I won't say. I may be a sad old gentleman, but I am a gentleman nevertheless."

"I paid," the King said again, but Aram refused to look back at him anymore.

Aram exited the cab outside of his apartment and walked up the stairs as fast as possible. His insides burned, and he waited for his immoral feet to catch fire. He would leave flaming footprints on the stairwell. He was nervous in a way that he hadn't been for years, but despite the fear, he was also energized. Never mind that he'd paid, that the Rat King had paid, he'd just bedded a firm young woman, and now he would go home and somehow make love to Sevart. They would stay up all night, talking about old times, sipping strong coffee and laughing. At dawn he would put on a favorite album, *Dean Martin's Best*, and dance, downstairs neighbors be damned.

But deep down he knew he would arrive to a dim, hushed apartment. Sevart would be dead asleep; she would hardly consent to being awakened, much less being made love to. There would be no dancing or coffee. Instead, he would sit in the living room, pitch dark except for the nagging pinlights, and he would wait until all the feelings - fear, lust, pride, self-pity - dissipated. And only then would he silently crawl into bed next to his wife, maybe put an arm around her. Maybe.

So he had half a heart attack when he opened the front door and found the TV blaring and Lori, in the track suit that doubled as her pajamas, curled up on the couch. On the TV was one of those reality shows that followed police officers. The officers were in the process of wrestling a man to the ground, and they were all yelling. Aram stood like a statue.

Lori took a moment to notice him. She rubbed at the corners of her eyes. "Dad? Where were you?"

"Lori? What are you doing here?"

She sat up and stretched. "I got into a fight with Keith."

"Is Keith your boyfriend? I thought it was Haig, the salesman."

"Haig was a jerk. I dumped him months ago."

"Why don't you turn down the TV? You'll wake your mother."

"Oh come on, Dad. You know that she can sleep through anything."

"But maybe I can't."

She muted the TV and suddenly there was just the two of them. "Where were you? What time is it?"

His well-practiced lie now lurched and fumbled from his lips.

"You went to the market for two hours and didn't buy anything?"

He stood frozen. Ready to confess everything. Ready to run out of that apartment and never return. Words choked up in his throat, and then he felt a small, hard plastic bottle in his coat pocket. "No," he said. "The truth is that I needed a drink." He pulled out the vodka, a relatively unconvincing gesture since it was full. He quickly put it back into his coat.

"Daddy!"

"I'm sorry. I was having trouble sleeping, so I needed a drink."

She crossed her arms, all judgment, but Aram felt relief because it looked like she'd bought his ruse. "I am sorry," he said again.

"We're going to talk about this."

"Not now, Lori. I am so very tired." He made a small show of heading into the bedroom, but she followed.

She reached into his coat pocket and wrestled the bottle out. "Kommissar Vodka? With a K? Dad, this is the cheap stuff. We're going to talk about this. We can't have you drinking while you're on duty."

"On duty?"

"You're mom's primary caretaker, right?"

Desperately, he took the bottle back, kissed her forehead and headed for bed. "On duty," he whispered to himself as his head hit the pillow. He put one arm around Sevart. He didn't know what to think; he was just a blank slate waiting for sleep. "On duty," he said one more time as though the phrase held some hidden meaning.

In the grey pre-dawn - after Lori had already left for her gym and while Sevart was in the bathroom - he took the bottle of Kommisar out of his coat again and poured most of it down the kitchen sink. He hid the bottle at the back of a shelf.

When Sevart came out of the bathroom, she said, "Remember we have dialysis."

He nodded.

"Where were you last night, Aram? Lori came over and couldn't find you, so she woke me up. We were worried."

"I had a drink."

She laughed. "I wish you had brought me one!"

Part grateful and part guilty, he let himself laugh with her.

In the bathroom - he didn't have much time as their appointment was for seven - he brushed his teeth. Then he opened the medicine cabinet to get shaving cream and found a scrap of paper waiting for him. Again the Rat King's handwriting. '*Meet me on the roof*,' it said. Underneath, the King's seal, a wax insignia shaped in a three-pointed crown over a rodent-skull. There was no time or date, just '*Meet me on the roof*,' but Aram suspected that he would know when the time came. Some signal would be sent.

As he lifted the razor, he had a mental image, a flash, of a blade. It was a magical weapon that he'd used, age ten, the last time he'd vanquished the Rat King. Was it real? It seemed impossible that the blade could exist, but he had a very clear picture in his head. A short, razor-sharp samurai sword with a gem-studded handle. Quite real. Or had it been a plastic children's toy? Or had it been a dream? And if it were real, where would it be? In their basement storage unit? Buried in the backyard of his childhood home? He had no idea where to begin looking for such a thing. *Forget the sword*, he told himself. *We have dialysis.*

Week in and out, he watched Sevart's blood flow silently, the pump on the machine spinning with a whisper. Sevart slept, and he was okay with her sleeping. Let her sleep. One of the attendants cleaned a machine in preparation for the next shift. The woman with the portable DVD - she must have been on the same shift as Sevart - watched another movie, and every once in a while a stray flicker of dialogue leaked from her headphones, but other than that, the room stayed silent. He kept an eye on the door, but the Rat King did not come.

As they climbed into their taxi, Sevart said, "Aram, we should go to church."

"Oh," he said. Doing the math in his head, he figured they hadn't been in nearly twelve years, not since a distant relative's christening.

"Church is a good place to go," the driver, a tall man with a distinct Haitian accent, offered.

"It is good," Aram said mostly to be polite. The truth was that, the times he'd gone, his favorite activity had been studying stained glass windows.

"We have problems. And church would be a good place to discuss problems. Maybe with the Reverend Mike."

"If Reverend Mike is still there." He spoke softly in an attempt to keep the driver out of their conversation. "Sevart, things may seem bad now, but I know that, pretty soon, you will be at the front of the donor list and you will get a new kidney. Very soon."

"It is not about the kidney," she said. "It's about the other night."

"I had some drink. It won't happen again."

She gave his hand a soft squeeze. "It is not the vodka, either. Listen, Aram, I know that you are not telling me the truth. You are avoiding something. It's like that time that you were laid off and you waited almost two weeks before you said anything."

He shrugged his shoulders, still embarrassed about that layoff twenty years later, and then he remembered Kelly's swaying breasts, and suddenly there was plenty more to be embarrassed about. "Maybe we should go to church," he said in a dry voice.

"I have been laid off too," the cab driver said by way of sympathy. "It's never easy for a man."

"We'll go Sunday," Sevart added. "Lori said she might come too. It was her idea."

Saturday night, a terrific windstorm hit. It knifed limbs off trees, temporarily knocked out their power, and sent the trash barrels dancing, dervish-like. Aram heard a harsh scratching from above, as though some piece of the roof had blown loose. He waited with Sevart by candlelight until the power flicked back on. Then they watched a figure skating program and shared, ticking off cups on the chalk board, half a pot of herbal tea. After she went to bed, he put on a heavy coat, tucked a steak knife into a pocket, and headed up to the roof. The storm had died down to occasional gusts, and the air was clean and cold. The Rat King was in his own heavy trenchcoat, and his hand-claws were gloved.

"What do you want?"

"Instead of answering yet another of your banal questions, let me ask you one. What do *you* want?" The King handed him a bottle of amber liquid. "Cognac. Relief. Relief is what everyone wants. Good cognac too. Not the cheap stuff!"

It dawned on Aram that the Rat King was drunk, the bottle almost a quarter empty. He walked all the way around the Rat King, in a deliberate circle. "Are you the Devil?" he finally asked.

"Ho no! If I were the Devil, I most certainly would not have developed this belly." The King patted his stomach. "I am the Rat King. What's the matter, Aram? You used to have no problem accepting me."

Very slowly, Aram reached out and touched the King's face. The fur there was short, and the texture reminded him of a lucky rabbit's foot. Aram thought this would be a good time for a swig of cognac. Aram had always been a lightweight drinker, but even he could tell that it was good stuff, smooth.

"Nice?" The Rat King shot him a grisly smile. "Do you remember when I raised Leviathan, the giant squid, and sent it to swallow New York?"

Aram nodded. The squid - he could picture it all these years later - had been vast in the Biblical sense, eyes the size of city blocks.

"Do you remember that you came on a zeppelin, and we fought on the unfinished skyscraper? Extraordinary, wasn't it? That was a golden age! Dueling, leaping across steel beams. You were my greatest adversary."

Aram remembered. The girders of the unfinished building occupying the same space and yet clearly distinct from his parents' old floral couch. He remembered the duel, swords crashing in arcs of blue steel. Finally piercing the Rat King's heart, sending him tumbling to his death. Diving into the harbor to retrieve Captain Nemo's Conch of Summoning and recalling Leviathan even as it began to devour the docks of Manhattan. He took another shot of cognac, let the heat melt down his throat. "I was a hero," he finally said.

"A grand hero," said the King. "And I was a grand villain."

"The best villain," Aram was forced to concede. "And do you remember the fight in the Himalayas? When I rode the white tiger?"

His head hurt. There was light and movement. He remembered peeing on the roof while the Rat King roared approval, walking - floating really - downstairs, holding his wife in a warm, drunken embrace before passing out.

"You were drinking," she said from somewhere above.

He opened an eye and clenched his teeth.

"I smell it on your breath even now."

He sniffed and nodded his head against the pillow, then closed his eyes and tried to go back to sleep. The cognac, this good cognac, had clobbered him. Was this the Rat King's agenda, to get Aram to succumb to whoring and drink?

What was next? Gambling? Smoking? It seemed ridiculous. Those were tactics worthy of an unscrupulous best man, not a monarch of evil, even a past-his-prime monarch of evil.

Sevart shook him. "Aram, we have to get up."

"Church?" he finally whispered. The inside of his mouth tasted bitter.

"Yes, and I'm glad Lori is coming because we need to have a serious discussion. I am afraid that I have been turning a blind eye to your drinking."

"I drank twice. Twice."

"You slept in your clothes," she said. "And I found this in your coat." She held up the steak knife.

"It was only in case..." But he wouldn't say.

"Tell me what's happening. Is it drugs?"

"No."

"You know that you can tell me," she insisted. "You know that you can trust me."

He nodded. Even though he understood that he shouldn't be, he was angry,. As a man of reason, he knew that chemicals, low-level alcohol poisoning technically, were the root of his irritation, but it didn't help to know - not for a moment. He resented being dragged to church to face Lori and this Revered Mike person whom, let's face it, they really didn't know from a hole in the wall.

"Will you tell me?" she asked again.

"We'll be late for church." He retreated to the bathroom.

Reverend Mike- his real name was Mesrop - didn't look all that different from twelve years before. He wore the same black shirt and pants. During services, which Aram found long and difficult, he wore the same shiny green cape. His salt and pepper beard had shifted to salt and sugar. "I have to admit," he said in Armenian, "it's been a long time since I have been involved in your lives."

"I'm sorry," Lori interrupted in English. "I'm out of practice."

"She really doesn't speak Armenian," Sevart said.

"Mom!"

"It's good to know multiple languages. For business purposes if nothing else." The Reverend Mike was known in the community as an advocate for keeping the old tongue alive.

"But we're not here about me," Lori said. "We're here about *him*."

Aram nodded. "My wife thinks my drinking could become a problem."

Reverend Mike nodded. "Drinking is not a good solution for our ills."

"And I think we need to talk about that, Dad. I just think you're having trouble dealing with the reality of Mom's condition."

Aram thought he would scream in frustration, and he might have except that the Reverend Mike turned to face Lori, and said, "You seem upset with your father."

"This is not about me," she said again. "My father is the one who's sneaking around doing who knows what and getting drunk."

"Nevertheless, he is your father."

Aram had had it. "I want to sleep with your mother."

"You sleep with me every night," said Sevart.

"No. I mean to have sex."

'Daddy!" Lori looked mortified, and it went downhill from there. The Reverend Mike tried a few times to get them to open up, but neither Aram nor Lori wanted to. Not at that exact moment, anyway. So finally the Reverend, in a quiet moment of exasperation, told them that he was very sorry, but it was clear to him that there were two different problems at play here. First, he noted, Aram and Sevart had needs, Biblical needs, that required frank conversation, and second, Aram and Lori also needed to talk things out in a civilized manner. Aram knew the Reverend Mike was dead-on, but locked in his hangover haze, he refused to give him even a nod of thanks. Who the hell was this guy, anyway?

And when Lori said again that it wasn't about her, the Reverend Mike told them that he would pray for them all and he had some pressing appointments, so if they would just leave his office, yes, the exit was right down that hall, he'd be more than happy to see them at some other time. And suddenly they were standing in the parking lot, raw and embarrassed to face each other.

Lori looked like she might say something, but Sevart put her hand up, and Lori let out a sigh instead.

"Let's go home," Sevart said. "It's cold out, and I would like to be in my home."

"I'll drive you guys," said Lori. Aram made a production of saying they would wait for a cab but, in the end, he was happy to sit quietly, shading his eyes, in the heated back seat of Lori's SUV. As they made their way back to Brighton, he thought that religion would not be the fuel that would save the marvelous engine of their marriage, not now. The streets were fairly quiet and, despite the cold, the sky was sunny. His hangover and the accompanying headache began to slowly leach away.

After they'd come home and taken off their coats, he saw that Sevart's eyes were red, nearly bloodshot. She kept her gaze focused straight ahead, looking neither right nor left, a sure sign that her feelings had been hurt.

"I'm sorry," he said.

"You embarrassed me in front of the Reverend. But I'm sorry too. Because we have not made love in so long."

"There's no need to apologize."

She sat on the couch, "But we're old, Aram, and there's this sickness." She waved her hands as if warding off evil spirits. "Makes me feel ugly."

"No need to apologize," he repeated. Then he added, "There is something. I was visited by an old friend."

"Oh?" She seemed to brighten up and actually looked at him. "Was it Sergi, the one who did the nuclear work?"

"No. You don't know this one."

"We've been married for thirty years- who don't I know?"

"From childhood." His headache seemed to have left him completely, and he suddenly felt as though things could get better. "This friend, I knew him in school, but he's a troublemaker. He's the one who I've been meeting for drinks."

"Well, maybe you can invite him over. He can come for dinner. That way you could drink wine at the table like civilized people."

"I don't think so. I don't think that would be a good idea." And then he didn't know what to say to Sevart's blank stare, so he added. "He is involved in trouble. He is trouble."

Sevart didn't reply. She just sat on the couch and gave him a look. Aram knew that she could sense his lies and flimflam excuses.

"I have some cleaning to do." She went to the corner, something she hadn't done in months, and began to detach the rechargeable vacuum from its dock.

"Let me help you," he said - the vacuum was heavy and hard on the arms - but she stood in such a way that he couldn't help. As Aram watched her, he understood that he'd had a chance to confess. Maybe a chance to save their marvelous engine, but for God's sake, how could anyone explain the Rat King? He retreated to a corner and watched his wife vacuum.

"I heard you went to church," said the Rat King.

"From whom did you hear that?"

"From church mice!" The King laughed at him. "Get it?"

Aram didn't move. He kept a poker face, but the truth was that he was terrified. This was the first time that the Rat King had shown up in their home. With Sevart in the next room, he feared for their lives.

"What are you watching?"

"It's about the history of bluegrass music, but mostly I keep the TV on for background noise while I read the paper."

"Bluegrass music," the King said in a blank way that suggested he'd never heard of such a thing. "I don't have a television myself. I don't understand these newfangled marvels. They seem miraculous, no?" The Rat King chewed on his bottom lip with a look that Aram interpreted as wistful.

Here in his home.

"Aram," Sevart called out from the bathroom, "Are you calling me?"

"No, no. I'm talking to myself - I'm talking to the TV!"

"Is it talking back to you?"

The King looked embarrassed, as though he'd been caught. "I'm sorry about your wife."

"Then leave. You're causing problems. Just go away."

"I can't, you bastard!" The King's opened his mouth just wide enough to expose jagged fangs, serving as a reminder of the animal inside. "You keep bringing me back."

In the bathroom, the noise of running water suddenly stopped. He could hear the door creaking open.

"I will be short," said the Rat King. "I won't tarry. Here is a ticket by aircoach to Las Vegas." The ticket that he produced looked legitimate, with barcodes and safety warnings.

"What am I going to do with this?"

"Sometimes you're frustratingly obtuse, Aram," was what the Rat King said before he stepped into the front hall and vanished utterly.

"Aram."

For a second, he had no idea who could be talking to him.

Sevart was wearing her pink cotton bathrobe. "Please come to bed."

He followed her, and she took off her robe. Her body was round, softened with age in some places as if to compliment the parts of Aram that had gone hard and craggy over the years. Her fistula stood out on her arm. Yes, it had been a long time since they'd had sex, but he still knew her form intimately, and he very much hoped for an erection, but his cock didn't always work the way it should anymore. So he took off his clothes, regarded his tired-looking genitals, took Sevart in his arms and told her that her loved her. They held each other, warm and naked, for hours, dozing occasionally, sometimes talking about old times - they remembered a story of how in sixth grade, Lori had stolen a friend's pet mouse - and he still didn't get an erection, but Sevart said it was all right and that someday soon they might do this again, and then he would get one, and they would make love, and it would be all right.

"It's important that we tried," Aram said.

"Does this help?" she asked.

"It helps."

"Will you talk to Lori? It's been a while since you spoke to her."

"I should."

"Thank you," she said.

He kissed her hand.

Then she said, "Have you seen your friend?"

"Melbourne? I'm seeing him Tuesday."

"No. The other one. The troublemaker ."

"No, no. He's gone."

"Thank you for telling me about him."

"I'm sorry too," he said, "that I couldn't tell you more."

"Maybe I should tell *you* something," Sevart said.

"What is it?"

Instead of answering, she pulled her pastel sketchpad out from under the bed and showed him the completed drawing, the *American Gothic,* but it was no longer that painting at all. There were two old people, and judging from the woman's rotund figure and large breasts, and the man's glasses and sharp nose, it was meant to be a portrait of the two of them. In the drawing, they stood in a flowery garden, flanked by sun and blue sky and what appeared to be giant butterflies and moths. She'd covered the grey lines with layers of healthy pink and yellow. The couple smiled. Behind them was a mountainous landscape which followed the line that Aram had mistaken for a cave or umbrella before. She'd given the mountains a Tyrolean quality, green with small white flowers, and on, completely out of scale, were pan-like creatures, mountain goat from the waist down and human above. The pan-like creatures were drawn dancing, prancing and playing their pipes.

"It's very fantastical," he said.

"Well, not everyone can be a hardheaded realist like you," she said in a loud way to let him know that she was poking fun at his background in engineering.

"This drawing, it's beautiful," he said, and he meant it.

"Does it remind you of something?"

Before he could think of better words to express his feeling, he said, "It reminds me of happier times in the past."

She took the pad from his grasp. "Or happier times to be." It occurred to him that the optimism he saw in this drawing might be the fuel to save their marriage. If he could find a name for such optimism. If he could bottle it and drink it down. If it wasn't for the damn Rat King.

Melbourne tugged at his fuzzy beard and ordered some fancy German ale.

"Coffee," Aram said.

"No beer for you?"

Aram shook his head. "I've been drinking too much as of late."

"In trouble with the lady?" And when Aram didn't answer, Melbourne said, "I'm only joking. How is she?"

"She's maintaining - doing well. We hope she remains healthy until-"

"Until the new kidney."

They'd been through the kidney conversation a few times before, so Aram decided to change subjects. "I was thinking about going to Las Vegas," he said. "What do you think?"

"We were there for a convention. Remember? Weren't we? Eighty-three, I think? Well, some time in the eighties."

"But that was business. I don't even remember leaving the hotel." Aram conjured up a dim memory of some huge convention hall, rooms that had been covered in ugly, beige flooring with the insect-like parts of dissected light planes and their engines. Salesmen in their navy blazers, making small talk and handing out flyers. Other than a small cluster of slot machines near the entrance, they might have been anywhere.

Melbourne cocked his head. 'Well, Vegas is supposed to be more touristy now. Palatial hotels and all that. Lots of restaurants and shows. You remember Gil Lynch?"

"From Sales?" Aram carefully took his coffee - they made it extra hot here - from the waitress.

"Back in a minute," she told them.

Foam settled onto Melbourne's beard as he took a preliminary sip of his beer. "He went out to Vegas for his birthday last year. He said he had a great time. Plus it's hot out there in the desert, so that beats all."

"Warm."

"Yes. Good for the old joints. You and Sevart should go."

Aram took a breath. "Well, the problem is that I only have one ticket."

Melbourne gave him a blank look.

"I won one ticket from a radio show."

"That's a pretty lame prize." Melbourne chuckled to himself and then said, "You know, hookers are legal out there."

Aram took a long sip of his coffee.

"I'm just kidding, Aram, but a guy could have great time out there. You could play blackjack all night. Sip fine scotch during the day. It's a fantasy land. Everything's open twenty-four hours. Plus they have girly shows. The old fashioned kind - with class, you know. Girls with big balloons and feathers. None of that dirty stuff. Hell, it's stuff you'd see in a movie."

"I'm sure I'm much too old for that. Maybe you should go instead of me." Aram stared at his friend and a cold feeling came over him. As though he was being watched. As though the Rat King was there, spying on him from a shadowy corner. But he looked around carefully and the King was not there - not that he could see.

"Another drink? Ready to order?" asked the waitress.

"Give this man another coffee," Melbourne winked at her. "He'll need it where he's going."

The next night, in the shower, he remembered the blade. He remembered how to find it. It was a simple affair, really. Like riding a bicycle- *once you've learned, you can never really forget*. It involved turning sideways to the universe. He did it naked, right there in the shower. For a moment, the bathroom seemed to wobble like the surface of water that had been disturbed, and then everything shifted. Aram trembled with childlike satisfaction. The world was like wallpaper, all the depth gone out of it. Weight and shadow took on a sketchy quality, and he walked naked beside that wallpaper. Bending the fourth dimension to his mind, it was easy to track back to his parents old home, maybe a five minute walk, and there was the blade, waiting in the white void just outside of the world.

It was wondrous - over three feet - with talismans and gems hanging from the handle. The handle itself was striped black and orange, the blade was cold and blue and nicked in a few spots from past duels with the Rat King, and it rested in his palm so easily, as though it had always been there. It had to remain hidden, of course, so he went back to their condo and tucked it in the space between the walls. He twisted the blade just so, and then Aram himself turned and came back into traditional space. His vision unbent, and suddenly he was back in the shower again. "My blade," he said softly. He could almost hear the fine steel singing to him through the walls.

Later, he took a bus to Cushing-Parkhouse where Lori worked. The waiting room was firehouse red, like Sevart's favorite lipstick, with framed pictures of green peppers. A tall woman who worked at the front desk told him in no uncertain terms that he was not allowed to go into the back.

"She is my daughter."

"I'm sorry sir, but we have a strict policy. I already paged her, so if you'll just wait-"

"I just want to speak to my daughter," and for the second time he started down the hall. This time, the woman stood up and blocked the way. She was a good few inches taller than him and, for an angry moment, he considered shoving her aside. Instead, he stared at her, and she stared back, and they held a silent battle of wills for almost a minute until Lori appeared from around a corner.

"Dad?"

"*This woman* would not let me see you."

"My name is Claire," the woman said.

"I'm sorry," said Lori. "they're real serious about visitors. Let's go back to my office."

Her office was packed with file cabinets, binders and piles of loose paper. On her desk were two half-finished cups of coffee, a desktop computer and a laptop as well. Lori sat and crossed her arms.

"Why would this Claire not let me in? Did you tell her to make me wait?"

"No, that's just policy. She was just following orders, Daddy."

"So were the Nazis."

She rolled her eyes at him. "I don't think-"

"It's not a good policy."

"I don't make the rules, but I will, if you want, talk to the management about changing it, if you think it's unreasonable for your daughter to be safe from death threats."

"You get death threats?"

"Not me personally, but the firm does. We have an account with Planned Parenthood."

"The abortionists?"

"They're not *the abortionists*," she lowered her voice, mimicking him, "they believe in choice."

"That's what I meant." He looked around her office until he spotted another chair that was covered in a pile of loose paperwork. "Can your father sit down?"

She sighed, cleaned off the chair. "Did you specifically come to harass me, Dad? Because you could have saved time by just calling instead."

Once Aram sat he asked, "I am here because your mother asked me to talk to you. So why are you so angry at me?"

"I'm not."

"The Reverend Mike said you had a problem with me."

"Reverend Mike is a fat, patriarchal, white man."

"And yet it was your idea to see him. You told Sevart that it would be a good idea."

"Obviously I was mistaken." One of her computers hummed a small tune. "That means I have a meeting in fifteen minutes."

He could feel frustration creeping up and tightening around his collar. He desperately wanted to stand up, march out the door, take a cab to the airport, and get onto that plane to Las Vegas, and it was only his wobbly legs that prevented him from doing just that. Finally he said, "I came here to reconcile our differences."

"And this isn't about us. This is about Mom. About how you don't care for her."

"I'm with your mother every day. I drive her and cook for her and sit at the dialysis center."

"Well, I'm glad that you do what any loving husband would do, but there's a problem."

"There's no problem."

"You know she told me that she might move out."

He laughed. "That's the most ridiculous thing I've ever heard. First of all-"

"Look, Daddy, if the drinking wasn't trouble enough, she told me that she found a knife in your pocket last week. And now you're telling her stories about being mixed up with some criminal. I don't know which is worse, having a friend who's a thug, or using that as a lie to hide something else. Are you having an affair?"

Aram started to say something but then thought better.

Lori leaned back in her chair. "Look, Mom loves you, and she doesn't want to hurt your feelings. She asked me not to talk about any of this, but she can tell - we can all tell - that you're hiding something."

He swayed a little, shifting in his chair. "So she's leaving me?"

"She's not leaving anyone. She's thinking about staying with me until you straighten out your act."

"Lori. There is something that has troubled me since I was a child."

"Well, then deal with it."

"It's called the Rat King."

She held her palms up and out to show that he'd, once again, proven a disappointment. To show that he'd, once again, given her nothing to work with.

"Never you mind," said Aram. "I don't like your methods, but you are right. It is time for change. Lori, I know that you think I have been bad to your mother, but I do love her. I am there for her every day in a way that no one else can be."

"It's not just a matter of being there. Do you understand that Mom is dying?"

"She's not dying. You always have to be so dramatic. She's waiting for a new kidney. If she's good about maintaining her body and taking proper medication, then she'll stay healthy until she gets a new, functioning one."

"You act like this is one of your engineering problems."

"And you act like this is one of your advertising campaigns. One grand gesture after another. I wonder if drama will make your mother healthy?"

"Daddy!"

"And furthermore," he crossed his arms over his chest, "I have accepted your challenge. I will deal with this issue. I will solve this problem, so leave me be."

She put two fingers over her lips for a moment, as though she was smoking an invisible cigarette and suddenly asked, "But what's this Rat King thing?"

What was the Rat King? His childhood come back to claim him? His ticket to another life? His problem? His solution? But Lori's computer chimed again, reminding her that she was late for her meeting. "Can you find your way out?" she asked before he went.

After, he behaved so he wouldn't cause Sevart any more stress. He was agreeable. He tried to be cheerful about things. He did not know how to broach the topic of her moving out, so he didn't. Each night, after she fell asleep, he would brew himself a cup of Turkish coffee, make sure the mystic blade was still in its place, and then go up on the roof and wait. Three, four, five nights running. It was generally cold up there, miserable. One night he found a half-drunk college student who mumbled some sort of incoherent apology and left. Another night, he stood in cold rain, shivering like a dumb animal for an hour before giving up. By the fifth night, it was getting to him. Dark bags formed under his eyes, and he was groggy. During Sevart's dialysis sessions, he would start awake with no memory of having fallen asleep. It was on the sixth day that he opened his sock drawer, looked under the paper liner at the bottom, and pulled out the ticket to Las Vegas. Then he understood where and when he would see the Rat King next. He understood how it would end.

When the time came, he folded back into the fourth dimension, the world unwrapping like the foil from around a candy bar, took his magic blade, and headed back to the roof. There he attempted the spell for flying. He hadn't tried it since he was eight years old, but he was heartened by the fact that the fourth dimension had worked so well. He took a deep breath, raised his arms above his head and spoke the old words, and then he dove up into the night sky. Three, four feet. He pushed up until he was sure that he was indeed flying. A shiver of excitement passed through him, and he took a quick look around until he spotted a line of planes, which he followed to the airport in East Boston.

When he got close enough to the Air West terminals, he saw the Rat King. The King was wearing a blue baggage-handler uniform, a comically large pair of orange ear protectors perched on his head. He was busy loading luggage onto a truck, sometimes stopping to inspect tags. Aram lowered himself quietly until he was levitating maybe an inch or two above the ground. "You!" he yelled at the King, but the King didn't turn around.

For a second, Aram considered stabbing the Rat King in the back - it would have been easy enough - but he knew that wasn't how it worked, so he moved in closer and yelled again, and when the Rat King still didn't look up, he sighed in disgust and tapped him on the shoulder.

The Rat King leapt nearly four feet in the air and landed on top of the baggage cart. "Aram! You scared the soul from my body!" He climbed back down and took off his ear protectors. "You're flying! I didn't know that you still remembered how."

"You have to go."

"No, *you* have to go. Las Vegas awaits. Fun in the sun, so they say! Do you have your ticket?"

Aram pulled out the mystic blade. It glinted silver and white against the blinking runway lights. Still not allowing his feet to touch ground, he leveled the tip of the blade directly at the Rat King's nose. "You don't understand, King Rat. I want you gone. I have a family to take care of, and we have too many problems already without you hanging around and causing more."

The Rat King smiled, brilliant and sinister, in a way that suggested primordial beasts that we all fear, in a way that suggested the stuff of nightmares, and suddenly there was a war saber in each of his claws. Aram had forgotten that the Rat King often fought with both hands. The King advanced, spinning his sabers, one after the other, in a series of lightning-quick thrusts and slashes that sent Aram sprawling backward. Aram briefly considered fleeing, but it was too late for that; he took advantage of the distance between them to fly up and backward, and the Rat King followed at an alarming speed, skittering on all fours. Aram landed on the wing of a plane that was taxiing up the runway. He hoped the plane's movement might throw the King off his guard. Through tiny portholes, he could see the passengers making final phone calls before take off, strapping in, chatting with one another. None of the them seemed to take any notice of him- certainly an effect of the Rat King's invisibility. Then the Rat King hurled himself up onto the wing and came after Aram with everything - sabers, claws, fangs. Aram moved and dodged in ways that he had not since he was a small child. Yes, the magic was back, he could feel it. And they fought. They danced, weaved and attacked. Aram's glasses fell off, but he didn't need them anymore. The crash of their blades sent showers of sparks arching across the plane as it picked up speed, turned on its jets and hurled itself off the earth. As they fought - it was all so impossible - Aram felt himself growing younger. Vitality poured from a renewed heart into lean, strong limbs. And the Rat King too seemed to lose weight, his black eyes shone and his fur took on a youthful glow.

They fought on beyond the elevation where they should no longer have been able to breathe. Beyond the elevation where they should have frozen to death. And when the plane reached cruising altitude, Aram stepped off into upper atmosphere. "Come on Rat King - if you can fly."

The Rat King laughed at him. "I have a few tricks of my own, Aram," he called back. And he too stepped off the plane. At first, he fell and Aram hoped that the Rat King had made some stupid mistake, that he might get off the hook easily, but he could see the Rat King beginning to bob back up from below. What's more, the King seemed to be expanding like a bubble. Aram held a defensive crouch, not sure of what to expect; this was trick he hadn't seen before.

The Rat King seemed to unfold himself and his body took on the shape of a furry zeppelin, his arms and legs tiny vestiges on a superfat body, one that retained some vague semblance to his old shape. And by the time he reached Aram, the King was huge. Fifty, sixty meters long. His mouth opened, whale-like, to swallow Aram, and it was all Aram could do to dive down toward earth. The zeppelin-beast came after him. Rising drafts tore at him. He felt like he might lose consciousness, but there was nothing else he could do. He could feel the Rat King's breath, amplified a hundred times, over his shoulders.

The enormous maw came crashing down, and suddenly Aram was inside the blackness of the King's mouth. He landed against something soft and wet. There was an oppressive humidity and the smell was painfully rotten. Cursing, Aram raised the mystic blade over his head and brought it down as hard as he could into the flesh- tongue, gums, whatever it was- near him and he held on as the mouth opened in a deep roar and there was movement, a rush of air trying to suck him down into the belly of the beast. He was covered in saliva and the floor he stood on shook and vibrated, he thought his shoulders might dislocate, and he held on.

Then there was light, the mouth reopening, and he took his chance and dove back out. He flew back in a half-circle, passing below the Rat King's chin until he could view the dingy, grey underbelly. And he held his sword up and cut as he flew.

He heard the Rat King roar and at first he assumed it was a scream of pain, but he quickly understood that it was laughter. "You idiot," Aram hissed to himself. "It was trap, and you fell for it."

Almost on cue, out of the Rat King's rent flesh fell dozens of shadowy creatures shaped like the Rat King, but without feature. They seemed to be made of shadow, or maybe fog. And now the Rat-zeppelin seemed to split open of its own accord, calving a storm, probably hundreds, of the shadow beasts, and they swarmed toward Aram, but here the Rat King had committed a small error. Aram had seen this, the Shadow Army, before. He'd fought them in a pharaoh's tomb, and he knew they were susceptible to fire. He held his mystic blade high, and it glowed a deep golden-red as it caught the moon and starlight. The light become a flame and he lunged into the dark mass.

The icy claws and teeth of the shadow army clawed and ripped at his arms and legs. He responded by flying, spinning and weaving. He wielded his sword in a way that he hadn't in over fifty years. It became a superheated blur. He blinded their shadowy eyes. He decapitated, hacked off limbs and evaporated entire shadow beasts with arcs of flame.

He swung and fought until his limbs grew numb, until he vision swam, until he couldn't think, but there were hundreds, maybe thousands, and they continued to dive down on him, pushing him toward the earth. And when they'd driven him to ground, pain crawled up and around his body. He barely held it together, and he retreated until he was leaning against a boulder. He fought with just one hand because the other was too sore and swollen to use.

Somehow, he killed the last shadow beast, he wasn't sure how he'd done it, and then he could hear faint applause. Now unhurt and intact, The Rat King stood not twenty feet away. "Well, you did a fine job, Aram. I have to admit. It's like old times. I did not think that you had it in you to defeat the Shadow Army."

He couldn't stand, so Aram began crawling toward the Rat King. He spit violently, trying to clear his throat.

The Rat King looked down on him. "You know Aram, it's funny, but I had this idea when I saw you watching the television. Do you want to know what the idea was? Since you're in no shape to ask, I'll tell you. It suddenly occurred to me that, in fifty years of mortal combat, I've never tried one of these." He held up a chrome automatic pistol. "Can you imagine, all these decades and I've never tried a gun before?" As Aram approached, he aimed carefully at Aram's skull. "Do you see flashes of your life going through your head? I know I saw them when the time came."

Indeed, Aram thought that he might see glimpses of his life: his parents, Sevart, Lori maybe, except that he was simply too exhausted and too consumed with reaching the Rat King before he pulled the trigger.

In his sadistic way, the Rat King waited for Aram to get closer. "You really should have taken the trip to Las Vegas, Aram. I predict that you could have had a whole new life. Some young blond divorcee on your arm. You could have been free of those burdens you carry. It's just... so... sad." And the Rat King really did seem sad when he pulled the trigger.

For a second, nothing happened, and then Aram sat up onto his knees and thrust the mystic blade into the Rat King's belly. He pushed it in deep, until the Rat King's hot blood poured onto his hands and down his shirt. Then the Rat King's countenance paled; he was once more robbed of a sure victory. Aram could see the King's eyes slowly sinking back into his skull. Again, the King pulled the trigger and, again, nothing happened. "You have to release the safety," Aram croaked in a hoarse whisper.

The Rat King managed a faint, pained grin as he fell away to the ground. Not because he wanted to, but because he could no longer move, Aram lay his face against the King's hot, soaked fur. He understood that this was all simultaneously real and unreal. He knew that he'd nearly died, and also that his body was tucked, secure and warm, in a bed some thousand miles away. The fact that he existed in two places at the same time, however, was of minor concern in the face of painful exhaustion. He closed his eyes and a third consideration, a third place, came to him, that he and the Rat King might be simple figures in one of Sevart's fantastical drawings: sketchy, cartoony and larger than life. Their faces overrepresented in bold lines. A man laying on the corpse of a rat man in a bright green field under a shiny black sky, a pool of pastel red blood, and when he woke- when he woke for real in his bed in Boston- his back burned, his arms and head felt like jelly and his legs as though they were made of lead- he opened his eyes and looked to his wife. He put his hand on Sevart's back and said quietly, "Don't leave me."

"No," she whispered back. "No, I won't." Was she awake? her eyes were closed. Was she sleep-talking? It didn't matter, he figured, and he gently held her shoulders and fell back to dreamless sleep.

Author's Acknowledgments:

I would like to thank Pamela Painter, who taught me the basics of self-editing; Frederick Reiken and Uppinder Mehan, who guided me at Emerson College; Ryan Ballinger, Geoffrey Edelmann and Amy Helburn, all of whose careful readings of early drafts proved invaluable; Albert Barsoumian, who helped remind me of the Armenian language; all the good people at Last Light Studio; Leo Hamalian (RIP) for taking a chance on one of my earliest stories; and most importantly, my wife, Amy, who is there every day.

Made in the USA
Middletown, DE
12 May 2018